The Littlest Martyr

B. Billy Curtis

wearystone editions

DEDICATION

This book is dedicated to my mom.
With my heartfelt thanks to my editor, Jim Thomsen.
With my love and eternal gratitude to Dad,
Bob, Laura, Darrin, Matt, Willow, Grace
and my wife, life and inspiration Katie.

CHAPTER 1

I stole Cecilia's bicycle. That's how we met.

That was five years ago. I had just moved to this little town called Urbandale, Iowa. My mom and dad and I were going to be living with my aunt for awhile, until my dad got a job and got us a place of our own.

So there we were, and my aunt had just given me some speech or something about how girls should be respectful when speaking to their elders.

After ditching my family at her place, I walked for what seemed like miles, and I saw one identical house after another. All the same style and color, and all the lawns were perfectly green. Even though there were lots of toys in garages and such, the lawns looked like no kid had ever played on them.

I walked past one garage that didn't have a car, and I noticed a skateboard in there. So I looked around a bit and wandered inside to borrow the board for a test spin. I wasn't much at skateboarding, but I usually got pretty good at things after I practiced a bit. I didn't want to be seen riding the skateboard away from the garage, so I held it behind my back and went down the street a ways and around a corner and down a slope that led to a little reservoir. I put one foot on the skateboard, but I was a bit nervous about lifting the other foot off the ground. When I did, I balanced for a few good seconds, but the board went too fast, and I had to ditch it or end up in the water.

I stepped off pretty smoothly and didn't end up falling at all. The board, however, just kept on flying down the hill. All the way to the edge of the reservoir, where it balanced for a minute before falling into the water.

I shrugged and wandered on up the hill, and saw this crazy-looking old man. He pulled aside his curtains and gave me a dirty look.

"Quit staring, ya old creeper! Hey, what are you looking at?"

I yelled loud enough that I thought other neighbors would look out their windows to see what the fuss was about, but none did. The old guy shut his curtains, though.

I went on for another few blocks and started to think maybe I'd gotten myself lost. All the streets looked pretty much the same as each other. It felt like it would still be a couple hours before all the dads and moms were due home. But I was tired of wandering around, and my stomach grumbled, and there were obviously no little stores or gas stations anywhere in this neighborhood, no place I could jack something to eat. I was pretty much lost.

Time to find my way back to Aunt Jennifer's.

A couple of streets later, I saw an open garage door with a nice bicycle in there. No car, so the owner probably wasn't even home. It looked like there was a motorcycle under a tarp, but I wouldn't know how to ride one of those anyway. Even though I wasn't great on a board, I was wicked-fast on a bike, and I knew that grabbing it would double my chances of finding Aunt Jennifer's house before I died of famine.

Unlike a skateboard, I couldn't hide it behind my back, so I jumped on the seat and rode it straight out of the garage. I took a couple lefts when I should have taken rights, but eventually I came around a corner and found myself face to face with Aunt Jennifer's blue house. When I noticed the police cruiser in the driveway, I tried to duck my head and keep riding, but my dad saw me and yelled.

"OLIVIA LOUISE DRISCOLL! Get your butt over here."

The officer standing next to Dad was a woman cop.

I can tell you that Dad's face had always been kinda red. I guess it was just something in his genes or maybe he drank his face red with beer. But with how angry he was acting, and the way that woman cop's cruiser lights whirled, Dad's pudgy square face, with its rounded corners, looked almost identical to a hot ember of charcoal.

CHAPTER 2

All right, I'll admit that I've had some experience with cops over the years. Nothing big, but I got caught stealing a magazine from a drugstore once in Tennessee, and I was busted for truancy a time or two in California and Michigan and Ohio and Colorado and Florida and Oregon. And a few years ago a cop accused me of assault on a school bus because she tried to drag me off of it and make me walk home nearly a mile. Frankly, a ten-year-old shouldn't be forced to walk home a mile with all the psychos out there in the world.

One thing I learned through my experience with the law is that women cops are much, much, much bigger jerks to girls than guy cops are. A lot of times a man cop will take it fairly easy on a girl. You can always peg how you should deal with them based on what kind of a guy it is.

A by-the-book, ex-military guy cop will take it down a notch if you let the tears flow—guaranteed.

A nerdy, ugly-looking guy cop will back off if you say something like, "HEY! You can't touch me like that. Are you some kind of a perv?"

A nice-guy cop will take it easy on you if you're nice back at him. If you apologize and tell him all about how you're an at-risk youth who has moved twenty-three times in half as many years.

But the women cops ... look out.

They don't fall for the crying and they don't give a crap and a half about the perv accusation and they don't buy the at-risk-child angle.

I let the bicycle coast slowly up my aunt's driveway toward my dad and the lady cop.

"What's up, Dad?" I put a concerned expression on my face kinda like I had no idea why a police officer would be standing next to him. Even though I had a pretty good idea that the cop showed up because of the old creeper guy who saw that skateboard go into the reservoir.

"Where have you been, young lady?"

"I've just been out exploring." I smiled in his direction and neither of us mentioned anything about the bike I was sitting on. "Hello, officer. What brings you here? Is everything all right with Aunt Jennifer and Mom?"

"Your dad here was very concerned about you, so he called us to take a look around."

I stared at Dad and he shot me an expression that basically said, Just play along. I'll explain later.

"I'm sorry. I got a little lost. I didn't mean to be away from home for so long."

Dad came over and put his hand on my shoulder. "We were very worried about you, young lady. Scoot on inside for dinner. We'll have a little talk after we eat."

I leaned the bike against the porch and again apologized to the lady cop. Something was up with all of this, and I was totally confused, but figured I better get in the house and let Dad handle it. The minute I was inside past the screen door, I saw Aunt Jennifer was standing in there with her hands on her blue pants and she was looking right at me.

Aunt Jennifer wasn't exactly angry, but she wasn't happy either.

"Your father and I were very worried about you."

"I'm sorry."

"You know, at first he shrugged it all off and said you were an independent girl, but I told him that I didn't think I could allow such an independent girl to stay here at my house with me."

"I'm really sorry."

"I know you say you're sorry, Olivia. But I get the feeling you're the kind of young woman who simply says you're sorry to get the grownups to be quiet."

I wanted to say it again, of course, but I knew better this time. Aunt Jennifer wasn't as dumb as I thought; she was pretty tricky with her words.

"Did you make my dad call the police on me?"

"I didn't make your father do anything. I offered him some options, just like I'm offering you."

"What options are you offering me?"

"I'm offering you the option to straighten up and fly right, young lady, or ship out."

I was quiet for a long time, even though I immediately knew what I wanted to say. But Aunt Jennifer was obviously a witch and she was the kind of witch that wouldn't be fazed if I called her that. She was the kind of witch who didn't like it when "young ladies" and "young women" showed her up and taught her that she wasn't all that. It took a long time for the words to come out, but when they did come, they worked as well as I thought they might.

"That's a mixed metaphor," I said.

"What?"

"I said, that's a mixed metaphor."

She looked at me as if she had no clue what I was getting at.

"I was in the TAG program at my school last year. That's an acronym for Talented and Gifted so I probably understand those kinds of things better than you do. A mixed metaphor is when you use two or more metaphors that are incongruous or illogical when combined."

"What in the world are you talking about?"

"Straighten up and fly right, or ship out. One is a reference to airplanes and the other is a reference to boats. That's a mixed metaphor."

I could tell that Aunt Jennifer was totally pissed off now. She looked like she wanted to spit on me or something. Before she could say anything, though, there was a commotion outside.

"What bike?" I heard Dad ask. Somebody was out there with him and it wasn't just the lady cop.

I went to the screen door and saw a girl and a man I assumed was her dad. The girl was about my age, maybe younger. Maybe sixth or seventh grade. She pointed at the bicycle that I left by the porch.

"That's it. That's my bike."

"Yes, this is Cecilia's bike, Officer. It was in the garage about half an hour ago, and when we returned from the drugstore, it was gone."

This seemed like a good time to head on up to my bedroom, but Aunt Jennifer grabbed my shoulder.

Dad did a pretty good job of convincing everyone of my innocence, though. "Hmmm … it couldn't have been a half hour ago. Maybe several hours. Before she went missing my daughter found this bike abandoned out by the reservoir. I told her she could use it as long as she put signs up around the neighborhood."

I could see my aunt's expression out of the corner of my eyes. Her face was all screwed up, like she'd never heard of a dad protecting his kid before.

The little girl whose bike I'd stolen was mostly hidden from my view because of the rail on the front of my aunt's porch. But I could see enough of her to tell that she was wearing a skirt and a pair of Mary Janes. She was some kinda girly-girl, this Cecilia. And she just stayed there quiet and hidden behind the post while Dad convinced the lady cop that I found the bike.

"OK, so it's safe to say everything is sorted out here?" the cop asked, in a way that told me she didn't actually believe Dad, but she was willing to let it go if both men were happy.

I was looking at the back of Dad's head, but I knew what he was up to. He was grinning that sly smile of his that he always did when he first met people. Mom called it his crap-eating grin. The lady cop went on her way and Dad and the girl's dad started to talk to each other. I watched through the screen, and my aunt let out a big sigh and moved off into the kitchen.

I still couldn't see her face, but Cecilia was the kind of girl that you didn't need to see her face to get some sense of what she was like. She stood still and didn't fidget while the dads talked. She didn't speak herself, but I could tell by the way my dad and her dad kept looking over to her that she was the center of attention. Even though she didn't say a word and they weren't even talking about anything to do with her.

"New to Des Moines?"

"Yeah, we just moved in from Michigan. We're staying here at my sister's place until we get settled. You like it here?"

"Sure, it's a nice place to raise a family."

"Question for me is whether or not it's a good place to find some work."

"What's your vocation, Reggie?"

"I don't think I ever really had one of those," Dad said, and laughed. That was one of his favorite ways to endear himself to people. He'd act like he was a little slow—a little dumb, but not too dumb.

Cecilia's dad thought his joke was funny. Everyone does.

"What kind of work are you looking for around here?"

"I like a job where the boss trusts me with a little independence. Something where I punch the clock and go do my thing and nobody is standing over my shoulder the whole time. You know of anything along those lines?"

"Matter of fact, I work for Urbandale Parks and Rec, and they have another Gardener II position opening."

"Hmmm. Don't know much about gardening."

"It's just called that. Truth is I'm really an overpaid guy who mows lawns and rakes leaves."

"Overpaid sounds good. You have a business card?" Dad asked.

I couldn't see Dad's expression but I knew he was saying it with a straight face. He was kidding, but he said it as if he weren't. If the playing-dumb act didn't throw somebody, Dad would try the straight-faced joke and see if he could get a guy off his game. This one worked.

"Um … business card? Um, no, we don't have any sort of…."

When Cecilia's dad stopped short with his response, I knew my dad was grinning again.

"I'm just givin' you a hard time. What's the best way to get on with the Parks and Rec folks?"

I know it sounds strange, how I said just now that Cecilia seemed like the center of attention, but here's what it was like: It was like in a fairy tale or something when there is some sort of princess in the scene and you've got all these little dwarves running around and they have all kinds of crazy names like Goofy and Happy and such. Only, in this case there were two dwarves—Cecilia's dad and my dad—and they were pretty much Crazy and

7

Jack Assy. And it made no matter that they were doing all of the running around and drawing attention to themselves and acting the fools, because the princess just stood there and it was obvious that she was the one in charge. If she'd decided to say, "Flap your elbows like they're bird wings," there is little doubt that Crazy and Jack Assy would have done just that.

"Blah, blah, blah...."

"Blahddy, blahdy, blahdy...."

The two dads droned on and on and I kept trying to get a glance at Cecilia, but I didn't want to open the screen door and introduce myself or anything, given the whole situation with the bike and all. But I kept angling for a good line of sight. Then, out of the blue, like she had some sixth sense or something, Cecilia ducked down so that her face was below the line of the porch rail. And she turned and gave me a big smile.

It made me feel very nervous, that smile of hers. Made me feel like she could see everything about me when she looked at me.

"Hi," she said. "You must be the girl who found my bike."

Both dads quit talking and turned to look at me through the screen door and for some reason, something came over me. I was overcome with some sort of great shame or sadness or guilt or something or another. I don't know what it was, but I felt my stomach go quivery and the inside of my chest felt completely hollow.

I tried to speak, but the only thing that came out of my mouth was a gagging sound and then I felt tears crawling down my cheeks, and I exploded in a burst of sadness and ran.

And let me tell you, that was not the kind of thing I ever did before I met Cecilia.

CHAPTER 3

I should probably give you a little background here. I should also probably do a little foreshadowing. Hell, for that matter, I should just tell you straight up what the deal is.

I....

Wait.

I always see how people start their books with the word "I," but it seems like my story is a little different and because of that should start differently. Seems like my story is more of a "we" kinda deal.

We had to move a hell of a lot while I was growing up. From the age of zero up until thirteen, I moved over twenty-three times. Nearly twice a year, if you want to think about it that way. Every few months Dad would get fired or quit his job—usually after a real throwdown with his boss. Sometimes, he just couldn't stick with it because some N-word or some foreigner would get all the glory for what Dad had been up to. Of course Dad didn't say "N-word" when he went on one of his rants. Mom was the one that taught me that girls shouldn't swear, though I'd heard her say those words too.

I did lots of things differently than they did, though. I quit eating meat on my thirteenth birthday and, believe-you-me, my parents were none too happy about that.

"Listen here, Olivia. Don't think you're going to turn into one of them lesbians with a bushel of hair growing up under your pits," Dad yelled after Mom gave me permission to quit eating meat. And, to be clear he didn't actually use the word "lesbian" when he said it.

"Just because I don't want to eat animals doesn't mean I'm a lesbian, Dad."

I didn't actually say "lesbian" either, but that was back when I still said that stuff. I pretty much quit soon after we moved to the suburbs of Des Moines and I met Cecilia. Like my mom, Cecilia advised me not to swear and told me that people are just people and we shouldn't label them as n-words or f-words or r-munchers.

Though you wouldn't guess it from what I've said so far, Cecilia ended up saving me from a whole lot of crap that I had to deal with because Dad was such a negative d-bag and Mom just went along with him. Mom was a nice person, overall, but she'd never been too smart. She never went to school very much when she was growing up. She liked to watch her stories during the day, but she couldn't even get hired for a job. Dad was good at getting jobs, not so good at keeping them.

"Here's the problem with your mother," Dad once said. "She's a goodhearted person, but she's a little afraid of people, so she ends up not standing up for herself. She gives in too easily and has a hard time saying no. Your mother went through some hard times when she was growing up and some bad things happened to her. Let's just leave it at that."

Now, I knew all about the bad things that happened to Mom because I could put two and two together. I'd seen enough episodes of different TV shows and learned enough about the bad things that happen to girls at the hands of their grandpas and uncles that I figured it out.

Mom mostly just wanted me to pretend like problems didn't exist at all, which is probably the only way she'd been able to get through life.

"Now, honey...." Mom started when I got myself wound up about one thing or another.

"Now, honey ... you can just ignore those boys."

"Now, honey ... it won't do any good to fret about that teacher."

"Now, honey ... you better pull it together before your father gets home or he won't be happy."

The last one was true quite a bit. Not that Dad ever hit me or anything. I remember once he threatened to go after me with a belt, but that might have been something else I saw on TV.

Sometimes it's hard to tell the difference between my memories and the memories of some guy that wrote a TV show or a movie. But I do know for certain that Dad could be a complete-and-utter pissed-off jackass. When he was pissed, you better just run your butt out of the house and get hidden at the neighbors. He'd yell and scream. Spit would fly from his mouth. The veins in his forehead would stand out and look like rivers on a relief map. Little rivers of dark blood looked like they were to explode out his head because they were boiling hot. Like a pot of tomato soup made with milk instead of water, so it boils over when the burner is turned to six instead of four.

Cecilia would tell me that I should be sympathetic about Dad and Mom. She said that she knew they were doing the best they could with limited resources. She said it was important to love everyone and try to look inside other people for the good in them. Cecilia said that when we look inside others for their good, it makes it easier to find the good that's inside us.

But she never had to deal with Dad on one of the days before he got fired.

It was always the day before he got fired that was the worst. Usually like I imagined—that tomato soup on the burner turned up to six or maybe even eight. The anger spent some time building up steam and then finally it just knocked the lid right off the top and started bubbling over the sides.

That was the day before.

Then, on the next day, it was as if his boss said: "Reggie, I'm sorry but I have to let you go because you left the burner on eight yesterday and I can't keep mopping up after your messes."

On the days Dad got fired, he'd go out drinking all afternoon and get home and clench his teeth and complain about the n-words and the foreigners. But he just kept his teeth clenched. He didn't pull out his belt and threaten anybody with it.

The days after Dad got fired were when he'd start to scheming. He'd think up all kinds of ways he could get back at "them." He'd call his buddies (he always had a ton of them within a week or so of moving into a new town). Him and his buddies would come up with crazy plans about how they'd blow up the plant or drive a stolen truck through the window at the burger joint or mix up some powdered chemical or another and mail it to the boss that fired him.

But then, around the time Dad would start getting totally serious about doing something, all his buddies would realize that he was serious, and they had just been joking. So they would slowly stop coming around to hang out with him and drink with him.

When the last of his buddies quit coming around is when Dad would pack us up and usually leave the furniture behind. We'd move somewhere new where there weren't a bunch of n-word-lovers.

Dad was five feet, six inches with red hair, and I'd overheard some of the things his so-called friends would say behind his back. They'd call him a leprechaun or Napoleon or say he had "short man syndrome," which was supposedly some sort of psychological condition suffered by vertically challenged men. This condition apparently made some short guys want to prove they were tough so they were always picking fights with other people. Dad's friends joked as if this was just a made-up disease, but I often wondered if it was for real. It totally described Dad, and I would not have wanted to be the guy who called him a leprechaun to his face.

During the trip to somewhere new and during the first week or so that we got there, before Dad found his new group of buddies, Mom and I were all that he had. For that matter, Mom and Dad were all I had too. But that's when I met Cecilia.

After I stole her bike and all, my dad started working at the Parks and Rec and got to being buddies with Cecilia's dad and hanging out at the sports bar in that little strip mall by the Hy-Vee. Cecilia's dad was a real quiet guy. Nothing like my dad. Turned out his politics were pretty much the opposite too.

Mr. French was not the kind of dad who ranted and raved about foreigners. My dad was like that tomato soup that was sitting on the stove for too long until it suddenly exploded all red, and hot, and goopy all over the damn place. Cecilia's dad was more like a pan full of soup that had been sitting on the burner set to one or maybe at the most two. Only it had been sitting on the burner for a week and a half.

He was like the kind of soup that just slowly and quietly

hissed and never boiled over, but then you took the lid off and looked and there was nothing left. It was just a big ol' pot of burnt soup on the bottom and nothing else. Which probably explained some of the way that Cecilia was.

Cecilia was more like a bottomless pot of soup. She was like the soup you get at the all-you-can-eat buffet out on Douglas near Merle Hay Mall. She was the opposite of her dad. When you looked into Mr. French's face you saw little black pits instead of eyes. It was like he didn't have any soul at all. Sometimes I wonder if all the soul in the family belonged to Cecilia. Her mom died when Cecilia was a little girl, so all she had was her dad and vice versa.

She had blue eyes and long, curly, blond hair. She was a little smaller than the other girls our age. She wore lots of dresses, not because her dad made her like my dad was always trying to do. She just liked dresses.

That's one way that she was like the opposite of me. I had dark hair and wore it cut short. I pretty much dressed like a tomboy even though my dad tried to make me wear frilly crap and flowery crap. I don't know one way or another what my eyes looked like. They were kinda hazel, so I suppose they fell somewhere between Mr. French's eyes and Cecilia's. I like to think I had an average amount of soul.

But it wasn't only soul that Cecilia had a bunch of. Cecilia was extremely smart too. Sure, she liked to give me advice and tell me how to get by. But she usually didn't give the advice in a know-it-all kind of way. She hesitated and bit her lip right before she offered to tell me something. She would then ask, "Are you willing to hear some feedback about that?"

And sometimes, when I was too pissed off, I'd tell her "no" and that was just fine with her. She wouldn't bring it up again until I actually asked her what the advice was and then she'd tell me something ... something wise.

Cecilia was wise beyond her years.

But then again, I can't be 100 percent happy with how wise she was. Obviously she wasn't wise about everything. Obviously, she was dumb about some things or she would still be alive.

She was very dumb about things like not blowing yourself up

with a bomb and killing a whole bunch of innocent people just because your dad is a vegan, anarchist, soulless, black-pits-for-eyes lunatic.

CHAPTER 4

We had come from Novi, Michigan, where Dad had worked as a custodian for the school district. A couple weeks after he got fired, he packed us up in the middle of the night and we headed southwest. It was the middle of July. We often left in the middle of the month because that's when the landlord started making a fuss about our late rent.

When we hit Illinois we started seeing lots of cornfields. By the time we made it to Iowa, that was practically all we saw. Corn practically up to my waist. My dad chatted up a waitress at a little truck stop, talking about all the corn and how it seemed to get bigger the minute we crossed the Mississippi. "Knee high by the Fourth of July," she said. The other thing I noticed right away about Iowa was how much it smelled like cow crap. I'd been to fairs before and I knew just what cow crap smelled like. But it was like the whole state was the victim of one ginormous cow that crapped on everything. After awhile, though, I got used to the smell and there was something comforting about it. Something that made a person feel right at home, as strange as that sounds.

Jennifer, my dad's aunt, knew we were coming. But when we got there it seemed like she got all nervous and didn't really want us to stay with her. Aunt Jennifer looked everywhere but at your face. She was a round woman—it seemed to me like almost everyone over thirty who lived in Iowa was round. She was polite but jittery. I don't know if her eyes were messed up or what, but it more than creeped me out the way she always looked past your shoulder when she spoke to you.

"Here's the room that you'll all have to share. I'm sorry I don't have more than one room for everyone, but I just can't have little ones in my room and have me sleep on the sofa." She glanced over my shoulder when she said "little ones," which bugged me, but I didn't say anything. I just met the lady and she was already being unfair with me, but I figure she didn't know any other way to be. Dad warned Mom and me ahead of time that Aunt Jennifer never had any kids of her own and never even got married, so she just didn't know what to do with kids.

"I tried to sleep on the sofa once, but I ended up with some neck problems because of it and I'm sorry, I just can't. But if this little one here wants the sofa, that's fine with me. She can sleep on the sofa if she wants or if you want her to because you want some privacy in your room…." Jennifer's words trailed off there and she started to blush a bright shade of red. I think she was talking about privacy for Mom and Dad about "doing it" but I didn't bother to tell her that I was pretty sure they never did it anymore anyway.

Her house was nice and new and very, very blue. Everything in the whole place was blue. The carpet was blue and the walls were blue and she had dozens and dozens of knickknacks on shelves. Every one of them blue. There were blue figurines and blue candles and blue flower vases with blue flowers. Aunt Jennifer wore a blue dress and her curtains were blue and her kitchen cabinets were blue and I just kept staring at it all once I realized. It slammed into me like a big blue wave.

"Your house is very blue. Why do you want everything so blue?" I asked Aunt Jennifer and all of a sudden she looked right at me with a big smile. She didn't look over my shoulder and she didn't look toward the ground.

She looked directly at me as if some light turned on in her head and she said: "Well, Olivia…." and I was surprised she even knew my name. She said: "Different people like different colors and I happen to like the color blue. What is your favorite color?"

She asked me the question like I was a little baby. She didn't exactly say it this way, but she might as well have said, "Wuts your faborite cubber?" all baby-like and annoying.

"My favorite color is charcoal gray, but it's not the only thing that I own," I told her. "Just because something is your favorite doesn't mean it's all you ever have. My favorite food is Häagen-Dazs Peanut Butter Chocolate Ice Cream, but if that's all I ate every day, I'd die of malnutrition, wouldn't I, Dad?"

When I looked up at Dad, he let loose a big, deep roar of a laugh and when he did that, I knew it meant that Mom was off to the side cringing like she had just smelled a bad fart. I didn't want to look over in her direction, 'cause I had the feeling I was already in trouble with her and in some ways, trouble with Mom was worse than trouble with Dad. He might yell, but she would ignore me and not even talk to me for hours or even a day or so, and then ask me to sit down for a talk, and it was all I could do when we had these talks to not squirm right out of my chair and go bury myself in the backyard.

Mom's talks were painful. They all went the same way, which was to say, she wanted me to know how embarrassed she was by me. She wanted me to know how I always let her down … actually, a lot of times she spoke about how much both me and Dad let her down.

"Don't mind Olivia, here." Dad said to Aunt Jennifer as he continued laughing. "She definitely gets her spunk from our side of the family."

Aunt Jennifer went back to looking away and she shrugged and I couldn't help but think how she was anything but spunky. She was spunkless, in my opinion. Spunkless and blue.

We settled in up in our room and Mom told us all that she needed a rest. She lay down on the bed. That meant even more trouble for me. I was dreading the talk that would be coming. I started to feel a little claustrophobic in the tiny bedroom and I knew I had to get out and run around for awhile. That was always the first thing I did when we moved somewhere new—get out and do some exploring. The first thing Mom always did was take her nap. When she was done with the nap and I was done with the exploring and Dad was out finding a bar, she'd pull me aside for our damn talk.

CHAPTER 5

My mom was asleep when I got up to the bedroom, after fleeing my dad and Cecilia's dad and Cecilia. So, I turned and ran the other direction toward the bathroom at the end of the hall. I burst through the door and landed right smack-dab in the middle of my Aunt Jennifer's crotch.

"Whoa. Slow down there, little lady. What's the matter with you?"

I looked up and didn't know what to say, but I saw her expression change to one of concern the minute she noticed I was crying. I turned again, this time running back down the stairs and making a beeline for the back door. Cecilia and the dads hadn't followed me into the house, and I could only guess what they were thinking about me.

I ran into the backyard, and just kept running for a long time. I ran through the grass of the people who lived behind my aunt, then I ran through the yard of the folks across the street from that, and then through the lawn of the family who lived behind them. I did this for a long time and never seemed to run out of yards to run through until, finally, my legs felt tired and I noticed that I was out of breath. There was a little park bench in this one backyard and the bench was all surrounded by flowers and there was a little birdbath beside it.

I sat down and put my head in my hands and simply sobbed.

I couldn't even remember the last time I cried. Maybe when I was about in kindergarten or something I might have cried because Dad told me we had to move because he needed a new job. I'm not sure that ever happened. It was another one of those memories where I couldn't decide if it was my memory, or something I saw on TV.

I sat on the little bench in that yard for a long time. I stopped crying after awhile, but I stayed there anyway and it seemed like it was getting dark outside, and I knew I'd have to head back home before Aunt Jennifer forced Dad to call the cops on me again. I saw a little movement or some sort of shadow or something against the window of the house that the bench belonged to. I looked up and saw that same old man who'd given me the dirty look about the skateboard. He stood there staring out the window at me sitting on his bench and it was all of a sudden like the sadness was gone and I was pissed at the old perv again.

"What the hell are you doing now, OLD CREEPER!" I shouted. "Do you like staring at girls and kidnapping them and killing them? Is that what you like to do?"

I'm not even sure where I came up with the kidnapping and killing part. But it must have just been my intuition and it must have been spot-on because it worked. He shut his curtain and I wandered back home straight through all of the yards.

Aunt Jennifer met me at the door. She told me that Dad had gone out to get a drink with his newfound Parks and Rec friend. Mom was still in bed.

"I was worried about you," my aunt said.

"Must not have been too worried. You didn't call the cops on me this time."

She bit her bottom lip. "It must be really hard moving as many times as you've had to."

Since it wasn't a question, I didn't bother with an answer. I simply stood there in front of her and looked around a bit and then looked at her and then looked around a bit more.

"I know you never met your grandpa, but he was a lot like your Dad, let me tell you."

I was a little curious about this statement, but, at the same time, I knew that usually when adults start talking about dead relatives, there was little room for a two-way conversation. So I maintained my bored look and waited for her to tell me more.

My aunt must have understood my silence, because she laughed a little bit. "Aren't you curious why I say that?"

"What do I care?"

She laughed again.

"Your dad is like your grandpa and you're a whole lot like I was at your age."

I scrunched up my face in response to that crock of crap.

"I bet that excites you to no end," Aunt Jennifer said and rubbed my head. She said good night and went off to her room.

That night I slept on the floor at the foot of my parents' bed like a dog. Without a pillow, my face got itchy against the loopy, blue, oval rug. The rug smelled like an old lady's house and though I hadn't noticed that smell in the house before, I now knew where my aunt was headed. Give it another couple years and her whole house would smell like that.

At some point, I remember waking up and the odor was suddenly overpowered by the smell of Dad. He smelled like beer and cigarettes and he grunted as he tripped over my ankle, then he landed in bed and I heard him rustling the covers trying to get all affectionate with Mom, who simply said, "No." A few minutes later, Dad was farting and snoring and sleep-scratching and to me it was like the sound of crickets lulling me to sleep.

For the next few days—or maybe it was even weeks, I don't know really—I pretty much became just like Mom. I mostly just hung around the house all day and didn't really do anything. My aunt was always trying to get me outside, but she wasn't the boss of me and she knew it. When she didn't know it, I shoved the fact in her face. Mom pretty much lay around all the time too. She took the bedroom and I lay around on the floor in the living room watching TV. The blue carpet down there was starting to smell like Old Lady House too.

Dad usually didn't make it home after work and didn't even bother to call to say he would miss dinner. My aunt asked Mom if that was usual and Mom just shrugged. I felt a little embarrassed for her because it was the usual and that it was not supposed to be the usual.

At night I started to get sick of the tripping and farting and snoring and sleep-scratching so I began sneaking down to the living room to sleep after I heard my aunt head off to her room.

I didn't see Cecilia again anytime soon, but I figured at some point we'd meet up. Dad always started off going to the bars with his new friends in town, but eventually he'd start bringing his friends and even their families around our house because the beer was cheaper. I thought I'd have to wait until we found our own place before he started doing that, but I had one of the rudest awakenings of my life when my aunt and my dad called a family meeting one Saturday morning.

"Olivia, we have something important to talk to you about." Dad said and then he looked over toward my aunt as if checking to see if he'd said it right.

Mom just sat off in the corner of the living room in this little chair, kinda all by herself while Dad spoke and Jennifer looked on with all matter of earnestness.

"We have some kind of good news, sort of, Olivia and I wanted to tell you about it and a decision that your mother and aunt and I came up with."

I knew from the get-go that this meant trouble, but I acted cheery anyway. Sometimes that's the best way to face this kind of thing. "What's the good news?"

"Well ... the good news is that I've ... we've ... found an apartment. It's not a whole house, so it's only a temporary thing until I get some more money saved from my Parks and Rec job. But it's a nice little apartment and it's only a few blocks from here."

"Okay, so what's the decision all about?"

"Well ... the thing about this apartment is that it's really small. It's just a studio apartment and I know how lately you haven't liked sharing the bedroom with Mom and me and that's only natural. You're getting older and it doesn't seem right to make you share a little apartment with us like that, so your aunt came up with an idea that...."

The rest of what Dad had to say just blended into a droning mechanical buzz. My aunt wasn't exactly smiling, but she had that kind of pursed-lip expression that told me that she was behind all this and she knew I wouldn't like it, but she was going to make this happen whether I liked it or not.

And Mom was too stupid and wimpy to do a damn thing about it, and Dad, who I thought gave a damn, didn't actually give a damn at all. He sold me out. I was only twelve years old and I was getting kicked out of my home. I was being kicked out of my own damn family.

"… better if you had your own room here in Aunt Jennifer's house. We'll only be a few blocks away, like I said, and as soon as we can afford a house where you can have your own room we'll be able to…."

Just a few weeks earlier, some strange girl (Cecilia) thanked me for finding her bike and it caused me to break down in tears and run away. Yet now, this huge thing in a person's life—getting abandoned by my parents, being orphaned before I even hit my teens—and I didn't feel sad the way most kids probably should. Don't get me wrong, I was feeling something all right. On the inside I was pissed. There was an explosion building up inside me. I felt rage the way Dad felt it sometimes. It was like that tomato soup or hot lava or warm blood. Like what happens in a horror flick when the slasher swings the ax and a fountain of red sprays everything all over.

Strangely enough, though, while I felt all of that on the inside, on the outside it was as if the explosion had already happened. My skin felt like melted wax that had already dried and taken on a new form. The blood on the walls had congealed and become a sticky paint job in the background of the crime scene when the detectives came to investigate. The splatters had already stained the walls and all the scrubbing in the world wouldn't remove the marks. The kitchen was dark; the house was abandoned; plywood covered the windows; a NO TRESPASSING sign was tacked to the door; the front yard was overgrown with weeds; the entire block was slated for demolition; and a slight breeze blew just enough to slowly turn the pedal of a rusted bicycle that lay on its side in the middle of the block.

The fire that I felt inside flickered now too. And then, with nobody else even knowing it was ever there, the fire went out and a thin stream of smoke puffed up into the air for a second until the same slight breeze whispered that away.

CHAPTER 6

The good thing about living with my aunt was that I quit moping around so much. The first day my parents moved into the studio apartment, I became more like my normal self and I started getting out into the world again. Aunt Jennifer set up all kinds of rules like staying home for breakfast and coming back for lunch and returning for dinner, and basically I just said screw that and I did whatever the hell I wanted to do.

To her credit, at first, she didn't push it too hard.

I walked around the neighborhood a lot and I borrowed a skateboard or two and a scooter now and then and two or three bicycles when I needed them. But I didn't take Cecilia's bike again, even though I saw it in her garage almost every day.

I liked walking past her house because I just hoped that little bitch would be outside some day and I could tell her what I really thought about her. I'm pretty good at breaking people down and even though I knew she'd be a challenge, I was sure I could take her. If I couldn't get her psychologically, I'd take care of Cecilia the old-fashioned way with a knee to the gut and an elbow to her head.

Eight days in a row I passed her house and never saw her, but on the ninth day there she was. She was in the garage getting onto her bike. She wore a stupid-looking pink helmet and even though I was quiet, it was like she had some sixth sense that I was behind her and she turned and smiled at me.

She waved at me like I was some long-lost friend, then she rode over my direction.

"Hey, Olivia! How's it going?"

I sneered, but it didn't seem to faze her.

"Fine."

"Looks like you got a bike too. Wanna ride down to the reservoir?"

"Sure. Why not."

We rode pretty fast and frankly I was surprised that such a girly-girl could keep up with me, but she knew what she was doing.

"My dad said that your parents moved into a little apartment and you're staying with your aunt so you can have your own room."

"Yeah."

"Do you ever get scared in your own room?"

"What?"

"I mean, I just wondered because sometimes I get a little anxious being in my own room. It's far down the hall from my father's room."

"Don't you have a mom?"

"No, my mother died when I was five. She had breast cancer and they had all kinds of chemo and treatments for her, even some experimental stuff, but she passed."

"She didn't want to do the treatments?"

"She did the treatments, but they didn't work."

"I thought you said she passed."

"She did."

I stopped my bike because I was thoroughly confused and starting to get a little ticked off. "Are you screwing with me?"

Cecilia stopped her bike alongside me and smiled a perplexed smile. She looked up with her big innocent eyes. "Why on earth would you think I am screwing with you?"

"First you said your mom passed, then you said she didn't pass."

"I never said that she didn't pass. I always said she did pass."

I knew she was full of it, because I'd heard her clearly, but I decided to let it drop.

We rode on toward the reservoir and laid our bicycles down against an old log that was actually an ancient telephone pole that the reservoir designers wanted everyone to think was a washed-up log. We walked down to the edge of the water, and Cecilia took off her shoes and began to walk into it.

"What are you doing?"

"Just getting my feet wet. Hey look! There's a skateboard in there." She moved slowly until the water was up past her ankles, then lifted the hem of her dress and started to wade in further but the water was too high. It came up over her knees and was nearly getting her underwear wet.

"I guess I can't reach it."

"What? You're afraid of a little water?" I kicked off my own shoes and just walked right in, letting my shorts and the bottom of my shirt get soaked, and grabbed the skateboard. As I lifted it from the reservoir, something suddenly came over me. I swung the board across the surface of the water and sent up a giant wave that totally soaked Cecilia and made her drop the hem of the dress into the water.

I'll admit that when I did this, I was feeling a bit annoyed so I probably did it to get that chicken-shit bitch. But the second the water hit her, she just started laughing. And she took a swing at the water with her hand and sent an even bigger wave at me.

We splashed like this for awhile, and I presented Cecilia with the skateboard as a present.

"What for?"

"I don't know. When's your birthday?"

"Not until December."

"December what?"

"December 25."

"No way! Christmas?"

"Yeah."

"All right, then, I guess you can either consider this present your early birthday present or your early Christmas present. Whichever you want."

She couldn't ride her bike and carry the skateboard at the same time, so I offered to take it. But then it was difficult to walk up the hill with my bike and the board too, so I took the bicycle back to the telephone tree/log and left it there.

"You're just going to leave your new bike there?"

"It's not really my bike. It's just some bike I found."

I wasn't thinking when I said it, but I suppose I knew on

some level that I was telling her something about myself. Telling her some truth about the time I "found" her bike. She got a mischievous look on her face and smiled. I think it was a smile that told me she knew things about me that I hadn't even told her.

The wet clothes felt squishy and heavy as we trudged up the hill. As we passed the old perv's house, I looked to see if his curtain was open, but it wasn't.

"You know who lives in that house?" I asked her.

"That's old Mr. Crenshaw."

"Did you know that he's some sort of creeper that wants to molest and kidnap and kill girls?"

Cecilia laughed like she thought that I was joking.

"Seriously. The old perv tried to get me to come in his house a few weeks ago."

"Mr. Crenshaw? No way. What did he say?"

"He told me he had something that he wanted to show me and he offered me a hundred bucks if I'd come in there and let him show it to me."

"No he didn't."

"I'm not kidding you. He gave me the hundred bucks too."

"You went in his house?"

"Hell yeah. I'll do anything for a hundred bucks."

"Did he … you know … did he show it to you?"

"Yeah, but I told him I'd only look at it for twenty seconds."

"You actually looked at it?"

"Sure. It was totally wrinkled and tiny."

"Holy crap." Cecilia stared over at the old man's house.

"I told him that for another hundred bucks I'd touch it." But by this time I could barely hide the expression on my face and she figured out that I was full of it.

"You like to make things up, don't you?"

"What do you mean?"

"Like about my bike and Mr. Crenshaw."

"Who says I'm making any of it up?"

She continued on as if she didn't even hear my question.

"I'm curious about something, Olivia. Don't you ever wonder why some people like to make things up and other people don't?"

I felt my face turning into a frown. "What are you trying to say?"

"Oh, I don't care if people make things up. I kind of like it actually. I think it's pretty funny. I'm just curious about what makes some people one way and other people another way."

I shrugged and we kept walking. I didn't want some girl that I just met to psychoanalyze me, even if she did it in a reasonably nice way. I'd been psychoanalyzed before by school counselors and teachers and sometimes the cops when they picked me up for something or another, so I knew it when I saw it. Even when somebody was being nice about it like Cecilia was. I think she was telling the truth when she said she thought it was funny.

"I mean, why do some people like to steal and lie and things, and other people just like to do things like go bowling?"

"Bowling?"

"Yeah, or something nice like that."

She said the whole bowling thing very seriously and this really irked me as we walked along and I got to thinking how Miss Priss over there next to me thought she was all that. Thought she was better than me because she didn't make things up. Because she liked bowling.

You know how sometimes you can feel your heart beating a little faster and you can feel your face getting warm and then hot and you just know that any minute now you're not going to be able to stop yourself because your arm and fist have minds of their own and you are about to pop someone in the face?

That's what was happening to me as we walked along.

And before I even knew what I was doing, I dropped the skateboard and turned and took a swing at Little Miss Priss and it all happened so quick that I couldn't stop myself. It happened so fast that I couldn't imagine she saw it coming.

But it didn't happen too fast for Cecilia.

She barely even changed the expression on her face as she ducked her head, let go of her bike long enough to punch me in the gut, then grabbed her bike again before it fell to the ground.

It was a hard hit and I doubled over trying to catch my breath. She walked her bike four feet, leaned it against a tree, then returned and put her hand on my back. "Are you okay?"

I crumpled to the ground in tears. Second time I ever met the girl and second time she had me in tears. I sat cross-legged and Cecilia put her hand on my head and I expected some sort of apology, but instead she simply stroked my hair and told me everything was going to be all right.

CHAPTER 7

I invited Cecilia over for dinner at my aunt's house because I figured it would be nice to have some company. On the days I actually made it home in time for dinner, Aunt Jennifer and I didn't do much talking. The first week or so after my parents moved out, they would come over for dinner too, but then they quit showing up so it was just me and my aunt. I knew why they quit coming. Dad had started going to the bar after work and I think Mom was embarrassed about it, so she just stayed at her apartment by herself. She probably didn't want to answer any of Jennifer's questions about Dad and why she let him get away with drinking so much.

Of course, Cecilia and Aunt Jennifer hit it off right away. I knew they would and in a way it felt a bit like the two of them against me, but what the hell. It was still better to sit there and eat my dinner and watch the two of them do their chatting back and forth than it was to sit there listening to the sound of my aunt chewing her food.

"This is a magnificent pork roast, Ms. Driscoll."

"Well, thank you, Cecilia. You're probably just saying that because you don't get many chances to eat good home-cooked meals. Does your dad cook?"

"Oh sure. Father likes to cook, but he doesn't have a big repertoire."

My aunt laughed at the word repertoire. At least that's what I think she was laughing at.

"What kind of food does he like to prepare?"

"Oh, he's kind of a natural, raw food kind of guy. We have lots of vegetables, and everything is always organic, and he doesn't do too much that's fancy. Lots of sweet potatoes and corn and some things like that."

"That sounds healthy."

"My dad makes a mean Kraft Macaroni and Cheese with Spam," I quipped with a deadpan expression. Cecilia laughed, but Aunt Jennifer looked embarrassed.

Then she acted as if I hadn't said a thing. "Well, that sounds good. I didn't know that about your father, Cecilia. I figured him for more of a TV dinner kind of guy."

"My father doesn't even believe in having a TV, let alone a TV dinner."

"You don't have a TV?" I asked. I'd never met someone who didn't believe in TV.

"No, when my mom died, my dad said we should get rid of it. He wanted us to simplify our lives. His theory is that some of what is poisoning our culture is things like TV and fast food and cars and stuff like that."

"You don't have a car either?"

"No, my father rides his bicycle to work and we take the bus anytime we have to go somewhere far away. He has a motorcycle too, but that's just for quick trips that are too far to go by bike."

"Your father sounds like an interesting character," Aunt Jennifer chimed in. "Is he a religious man?"

"Mmmm … not exactly," Cecilia says, cutting a precise cube of pork roast. "He believes in God, but he doesn't believe in organized religion. My father believes that organized religion causes a lot of the world's problems. My mother's family was very religious and I think that's part of the problem. When she was sick, her family didn't like some of the alternative treatments that she was trying out. I mean she did traditional medicine too, but I think they were against my father having her do other things so they kind of disowned each other when my mother died."

"That's too bad. Does that mean you never see your grandparents on that side of your family?"

"Actually, I don't get to see either of my sets of grandparents because my father is estranged from his family too."

"Why's that?" I asked, but you'd have thought that I'd ripped a loud fart the way my aunt looked at me. It was apparently okay for my aunt to ask Cecilia all kinds of questions, but the minute I asked one, I was invading her privacy.

"Well, my father said that his parents were undisciplined people."

This time, Aunt Jennifer and I both looked at each other. It was not exactly an answer we expected and since I could tell that my aunt wasn't going to follow up, I took the lead again.

"What the hell does that mean? Undisciplined?"

"You know, I think they were sort of like roustabouts … I think." This was only one of about three times during her short life that I saw Cecilia without her trademark confidence. You could tell her answers weren't really hers this time around. She used the word undisciplined because her father said it. Of course, I couldn't leave well enough alone.

"Roustabout? What's a roustabout? They were in a carnival or something?"

"That's enough with the Twenty Questions, Olivia," Aunt Jennifer said.

I shot her a pissed-off look, but the way she said it had as much finality as Cecilia's punch to my gut earlier.

We mostly made small talk after that, and after dinner Cecilia asked if she could see my room. I didn't understand why she'd want to, but Aunt Jennifer thought it was a good idea, so I shrugged and went along for the ride.

"You don't do much decorating, do you?"

"What kind of decorating am I supposed to do?"

"I don't know. Maybe some posters or some touch that makes this your space."

"It's not my space, though."

"Sure it is. It's your room, isn't it?"

"No, it's my aunt's room. I just stay in it because I need somewhere to stay while my parents are abandoning me."

"I'm just thinking that if you decorated your room and made it your own, you might not feel so abandoned."

I didn't understand what Cecilia was trying to get at with all this, but it seemed to be just more psychobabble. Like last time, it was starting to piss me off, but I knew better than to throw a punch. Without thinking, this time I went for a verbal assault.

31

"What do you know about abandonment?" I asked.

There was a long pause when I asked the question and I think the answer came into my head about the same time it must have came out of Cecilia's mouth and boy, did I feel stupid.

"My mother died, you know. That's a pretty big abandonment."

I simply shook my head. "Listen, Cecilia. I've moved so many times that I quit trying to decorate my bedroom a long time ago. What good does it do to put up a bunch of posters and then rip them all down in a month?"

"I guess that makes sense."

We stood in silence for a while longer and looked around my blue bedroom and I took it all in as if I was doing it for the first time. It looked mostly like a hotel room, with blue sheets and blue wallpaper and blue curtains accented by wicker decorations, and wall hangings that could be classified as puke-inducing country décor.

Still, the room was nicer than a lot of bedrooms I'd had over the years. Usually I was relegated to what was formerly some little kid's room with dirty white walls scribbled over with crayon marks. A lot of times we'd move into a house and I'd go running around it and find my room and discover abandoned toys. Not anything good, mind you, but usually some little plastic thing or another that the previous tenant had gotten out of a gumball machine or been given with a Happy Meal.

My reminiscence was interrupted by one loud voice and two quiet ones from downstairs, and I nearly cringed in embarrassment when I realized who it was. Our dads had returned from their drinking binge, and as per usual, my dad was mouthing off loudly about something or another. After some time at it, he began shouting for me.

"OLIVIA! Come on down and say hi to your dad. OLIVIA!"

I rolled my eyes, and Cecilia smiled. "This oughta be fun."

We made our way downstairs and my dad stood there leaning against a railing, while her father sat calmly in a living room chair carrying on a conversation with my aunt.

Though I hadn't seen Dad for a couple of weeks, I knew what he had been up to because Aunt Jennifer kept me up to date.

Apparently, Dad had gotten involved in something called the Freedom and Liberty Party. They were the group that was always on the news lately complaining about illegal immigrants and rights for gay people and basically anything else where they had an opportunity to take away the freedom and liberty of other people. Of course, Dad obviously didn't see it that way. He'd always been of the mind that "those" people were infringing on his freedom and liberty because they were trying to get special treatment.

According to Aunt Jennifer, Dad heard about the Freedom and Liberty Party one day and saw where they were coming to Des Moines to try and drum up some support. They didn't have a local chapter and wanted to start one. Somehow, Dad got involved and was actually some sort of bigwig in the local chapter. He'd finally found a group of lunatic friends who didn't run away when he started ranting.

In fact, according to my aunt, the FLP was planning on putting together some huge protest or something down at the Capitol Building or City Hall or something and they expected thousands of people from all over the Midwest and Dad was one of the main guys putting it together. I guess it was better than just being some drunk with friends who thought he was crazy.

"There she is! C'mon down here and say hi to Mr. French," Dad told me.

Cecilia's father waved and seemed nice enough. I remember thinking back then that it would be much better to have him as a father than my stupid old man. Of course, that was back before I noticed the lack of soul in his eyes.

It was actually kinda funny that Mr. French would still be hanging out with Dad, since I knew from Cecilia that Mr. French's politics were clear on the other side of the pendulum or spectrum or whatever it is that a person's politics could be on the other side of. I guess I figured Mr. French and my dad were simply work buddies, but later, after everything that happened happened, I decided that maybe Mr. French was like a spy trying to infiltrate my dad's mind. Find out as much as he could about the Freedom and Liberty Party in order to destroy it.

"Mr. French here was telling me all about his raw food diet. It's quite fascinating," Aunt Jennifer said.

"Interesting if you're into that kinda pansy-ass stuff," Dad added. As always, he said it in a way that was kidding around and wouldn't cause any grief for Mr. French. It took a long time of knowing Dad before he started to get under your skin with his joke-jabs.

Dad gave me a big hug like he always did, though the hugs tended to be bigger and more painful when he was drunk. I noticed that Cecilia's father didn't do any hugging and she just sat down on the arm of the chair that he'd taken. From their body language, you'd almost guess that they didn't know each other.

"Well, I think it's fascinating, this whole 'raw food movement,'" Aunt Jennifer said. "Did you know that there are even restaurants now that sell this kind of thing? Wouldn't do you any harm to eat a little better, Reggie."

Cecilia and her father and my aunt started into this whole conversation about food and eating healthy and organics and a bunch of crap like that. Meanwhile, Dad and I just stood off to the side. After a while, he put his arm around my shoulder and turned and told me that he was happy to see me.

"It's good to see you too," I said and I really meant it.

"Are things working out all right here with your aunt?"

I nodded, though I wasn't a hundred percent sure if they were or not. I have to admit that it wasn't as bad as I worried it would be. I could tell, though, that my aunt was just waiting back in the wings for me to get some sense of complacency, and then she was going to make an attempt at whipping me into shape.

I curled in next to my dad's armpit and realized I missed the scent of beer, BO, and sport-stick deodorant.

We stayed cuddled up like that while the others acted all smart and proud of themselves for their intelligence on a bunch of crap about sustainability and food and how our planet was slowly eroding.

I noticed a shaft of light from a streetlamp coming in past my aunt's blue curtain and for some reason it reminded me of when I was a little kid. A real little kid. In the middle of the night I'd sometimes have a brief bit of being scared because I'd wake up in my bedroom or sometimes the living room, or sometimes just a large walk-in closet. Wherever it was, it almost always looked the same, like I said, with bare walls and not a whole lot of decoration or anything. And I remember this feeling like I was all alone and I'd get anxious and I'd cry out, but Mom and Dad almost never came in to check on me. Sometimes, when we first moved to a place, Dad would be up late watching some TV show because he hadn't met enough friends yet to stumble home drunk and start up with the snoring, scratching and farting.

When that was the case, he'd yell to me from the living room. "Olivia. I'm right in here. C'mon in."

And I'd follow his voice and trundle along in my little footie pajamas. I can still feel how they seemed so snug on my toes and how the rubber pads on the bottom made a little shhh-shhhh sound as I shuffled along on the floor. I'd come into the living room and Dad would be there drinking something or another and watching a show.

"Are you all right, sweetie?"

Sometimes I'd answer and sometimes I would just sob.

"C'mon over here."

And I'd climb up on the sofa and get in there right beside him.

He'd ask me: "Do you want me to cuddle you? Or do you want to cuddle Daddy?"

And usually I'd answer that I wanted to cuddle Daddy and I'd wrap my arms as far around his big chest as I could, and I'd hold him like I was the one trying to keep him from being scared. And sometimes, there on the sofa, he'd fall asleep before I did and I would stare at the TV and listen to his snoring. Then, before I knew it, the TV would start with a bunch of shows that were trying to sell some product instead of entertain me. I'd watch and think about how much I wanted a vacuum bag system to store my winter quilts or how great it would be to cook meat in a Lean Machine grill instead of the old-fashioned way.

CHAPTER 8

Things went south after a while.

Mr. French and Cecilia and Aunt Jennifer kept going on and on about the raw foods thing and all this other crap. Eventually Dad got sick and tired of all their talk and he started to say stupid things that he thought were funny but nobody else appreciated. After a few minutes of this, I think Cecilia's father was pretty annoyed by it all and he said he and Cecilia had to get going, that it was already past her bedtime and that it wasn't right to keep a little girl up this late. And the way he said it made it sound like he was knocking Dad for letting me stay up late. And then my aunt kinda went along with the whole thing too, like it was all Dad's fault that I was up so late, and I kinda felt sorry for him.

I wanted to cuddle him like I used to when I was a little kid.

It seemed like he was being picked on by everyone, and he wasn't doing anything that they weren't up to themselves.

He just kinda wandered off right behind Cecilia and her father, and he never even really said goodbye to me. Then I did the same thing to my aunt by just wandering upstairs without saying any sort of good night. I had some trouble sleeping, but eventually I managed to catch a few z's. I'm not sure if I woke up scared in the middle of the night or not, but I guess it didn't matter because there was nowhere I could go even if I had.

I didn't see Dad again for another week or so.

At this point, I should also jump in here and mention that I never saw Mom during this time. She just sort of disappeared. I once saw a news story about some cop outside Chicago that people suspected of killing his wife because she just seemed to disappear one day. I knew better than to think Dad would do anything like that, but I do have an active imagination sometimes. I started to fantasize about what I'd say if the news camera crew came around and started asking questions about my mom who had disappeared. Started accusing Dad of killing her and burying her in cement or hacking up her body into tiny pieces so they couldn't be found.

I know this sounds coldhearted, but I didn't really miss Mom very much. She was barely there even when she was there, if you know what I mean.

Cecilia and I started to hang out a lot during that time, and that's when I learned that she had a mischievous streak too. It may seem like the way I talk about her she was all perfect and innocent and goody-two-shoes, but she liked to have fun as much as the next guy. It's just that she was pretty particular about what she would and what she wouldn't do for the fun.

For example:

She would not steal anything herself, but sometimes she found it pretty funny when I stole things.

She carried spiders outside and set them free, but laughed hysterically one time when I caught a fly in my hand and then ate it on a dare.

She almost never swore and always encouraged me not to call people swear words, but once when we went down to the Walgreens and stood in line behind this nervous high school guy, Cecilia nodded her head at him and said "hi" and pursed her lips the way folks do when they're passing the time. Then she looked down at the box of condoms in his hand and nodded and out of nowhere said, "Good day for doing a whole lot of screwing, huh?"

The guy was totally embarrassed and what cracked me up the most was how she said it as a joke to crack me up, but she didn't laugh herself until we got out of the store. Also, the way she chose the word "screwing" instead of any other word. It was hilarious.

One day we were hanging around outside the Casey's General store out on 100th. I was eating some biscuits and gravy, and she was chewing on an apple slice from one of those packages of apple slices that you buy from the section of the cooler next to the hardboiled eggs and mini-carrot nubs.

We were just sitting there on a yellow curb enjoying the day and watching folks come and go. This big pickup truck comes flying into the parking lot and it was like the guy driving it didn't even see us sitting there. He comes screaming into the parking space right in front of the curb where we were sitting. I swear the front bumper of this big truck was three inches from both our faces before this fat old construction dude in an orange vest with food stains all over his big fat belly jumps out of the truck. Then he throws a cigarette on the ground right next to us and runs into the store.

I was totally shocked and my heart was beating so fast you could probably see my shirt bumping in and out. And then I was so pissed. I was ready to jump up and run into the store and tell off this fat jackass who practically killed Cecilia and me. But when I looked over at Cecilia, she was just sitting there with a big grin on her face.

"What the hell are you smiling about?"

"Didn't you see that? That guy in the truck practically ran us over."

"Of course I did. How could I miss it? What is so damn happy-causing about that?" I didn't mean to say something as stupid as "happy-causing" but that's how the words came out, so I didn't try to correct them or say something smarter.

"He didn't run us over. That's the point. We could have been killed just now, but something happened that caused him to put the brake on just in time and here we still are eating our breakfast and we don't even have any scratches on us."

"But Cecilia, you can't just sit there all happy because you didn't get killed. The fact is that this stupid a-hole is going through his life either totally unaware of other people or aware that we were sitting there, but not caring that he almost killed us. Either way, this is nothing to be happy about. I have a good mind to go in there and tell him off."

"You can go tell him off if you want. I'm just happy because it seems like good news that my time has not come yet."

"Your time to die, you mean? What kind of stupid answer is that to a situation like this? The only reason it's not your time to die is because we lucked out right there. We could both be lying on the pavement right now with our heads caved in."

"But we're not, Olivia. Don't you see? We're not. We're still just sitting here on this same curb. Only now there's a big truck bumper six inches from our face and our legs are under this truck."

That's when I noticed that we were.

We were sitting there in the same spot and the truck's bumper was inches from our faces (though I still think it was more like three and not six).

I turned my head and stared at her and thought about how ridiculous it was that we were having this argument. Then the fat idiot came out of the store and he sort of slowed down when he saw us there and he gave us this funny look like, What are these two girls doing sitting on this curb with my bumper three to six inches from their faces? This doesn't make any sense. Hmmm....

Then, he simply got in his truck and backed out of the parking space and drove away as if nothing had happened.

I wasn't pissed for much longer and I certainly wasn't pissed like the time I tried to punch Cecilia out, but I guess you could say it irked me. It irked me the way Cecilia thought it was so cool to be so different. She always wanted to be smarter than me and she always acted like she was all that. One thing I learned though, while I was moving around so much, was that you kind of take your friends where you get them and as far as my long list of friends goes, Cecilia was far and away better than the rest. She was much smarter and much funnier and much more interesting to be around.

Most places I lived, I learned pretty quickly that when you're the new kid in town, you pretty much have to start at the bottom of the evolutionary scale when it comes to friends. Sometimes you get lucky and the new next-door neighbor is one of the popular kids in a town or at a school, but that was pretty rare in the ghetto neighborhoods that we mostly moved into. It was usually the rich kids who were popular, so that meant I started out at the bottom of the barrel. My first days in most schools involved sitting at the lunch table with the girls who ate their own boogers or sometimes ending up at a table with a bunch of boys that thought the funniest thing in the world was to see how loudly they could burp between arguments about manga and video games. After a few weeks sitting at a table with this group of losers, if I was lucky I'd move my way up the social ladder one rung or two before I had to move again.

Not that I wanted to hang out with phony popular kids or anything, but it might have been nice to find a compromise between booger-eaters and rich kids.

I usually had better luck when I moved into a town during the summer because school wasn't going on and then you simply make friends with the others in your neighborhood. Neighborhoods are more like families, where folks have to like each other because they had to live together. But lots of times, the minute school started, your neighborhood friends would abandon you at school if they considered themselves members of a higher caste than you.

The other thing about the neighborhood friends was that until you actually got into school with them, you couldn't be sure where they stood in the school social order.

I'd had neighborhood friends who were the coolest, suave, popular kids in the neighborhood, and then we got to school they were pretty much booger-eaters.

With all that in mind, I was very curious to find out where Cecilia fit into the scheme of things at school. Was she going to be one of the popular girls or was she going to sit at a table of booger-eaters? The one thing I didn't worry about was that she'd be the kind of girl who'd abandon me when we got to school. She seemed more loyal than that.

On the first day of school I asked her to walk with me and she said that she couldn't because she had to be at school early. She was an "Ambassador," whatever that meant.

Then, when I got to school, she was standing on the front stairs of Urbandale Middle School with a clipboard in her hand and a nametag that said J-Hawk Ambassador. Apparently, she was some sort of greeter for the kids and her job was to help direct them to their homerooms and lockers and classes throughout the day. When I arrived, there were people all over the place. It was strange. It seemed as if my whole summer was spent with just Cecilia and we were the only two kids in all of Urbandale. Now, here I was approaching the school and kids were coming from every damn direction.

I felt dizzy with all these people running around surrounding me on all sides. Then I felt a little sick to my stomach. Then I felt like I wanted to run the other way and go back to my aunt's, but of course that wouldn't do. I could go to Casey's General Store. I could go down to Merle Hay Mall and hang out for the day.

I noticed that I was frozen in one place standing there like an idiot and all these kids were rushing into the school. Then I caught Cecilia's eyes at the top of the steps and she smiled at me and I started to move toward her so that I could say hi. She was smiling and I was smiling and I'm a girl and all and she's a girl too, but I felt like I was in love with Cecilia. I felt like I wanted to run up and hug her and maybe even kiss her, you know, like in some sort of a romantic way. I wanted nothing more than to have Cecilia take my hand and be my ambassador and show me where to go.

I was running up toward the front doors, but then some other kid stepped in front of me and asked Cecilia how to find Mr. Redfield's room and I stood there patiently waiting my turn and then that kid left and I was about to say something to her again and another boy walked up and asked about his locker assignment and Cecilia started helping him.

Finally, after about four or five kids, she had a break and I said hi and she said hi to me and smiled, but it wasn't the big way she was smiling at the other kids. She smiled with a kind of tight smile like she was humoring me. She smiled at me like I was some sort of an annoyance, and then the first chance she got to help some other kid, she literally turned her back on me and started giving directions to the gym.

"Stupid bitch."

I turned and stormed off to spend the day at Merle Hay Mall.

CHAPTER 9

It was touch and go there for few days. I guess the school didn't know I wasn't showing up, or else it took them a few days to get around to calling my family. I left the house each morning and went off to the mall, or sometimes to Beaverdale. Once I took the bus all the way to the fairgrounds. Each day that I was truant, I thought I'd get home and my aunt would ream me a new one, but each day I just arrived and she asked me how school was and I told her it was great and made up some good names for the teachers and came up with crazy stories about kids that didn't really exist and generally did a good job of faking my way through the week.

Cecilia called my aunt and stopped by a few times looking for me, but I told Aunt Jennifer I didn't want to talk to her, so I just hung out in my room or around the corner from the front door so Cecilia couldn't see me. My aunt would tell Cecilia, "She says she doesn't feel like company right now," even though I'd asked her to say I was sick or I was not here. But Cecilia didn't press it, so all was okay.

I have to give credit to Cecilia too.

When my aunt asked her, "Didn't you see her at school today?"

Cecilia would answer, "We're not in any of the same classes," which was true, I suppose.

I never knew which classes I was supposed to be in, because even before I arrived, I hadn't seen a class schedule or anything else. As my second week of skipping school started, this whole situation got me to thinking. So, one night at dinner I tried to bring up a casual question:

"Aunt Jennifer?"

"Yes, Olivia?"

"I have a weird thing to ask you."

"Sure, what is it?"

"Well, I was just wondering if you were the one who signed me up for school, or if my mom or dad did it."

She gave me a puzzled look, so I knew I better come up with an excuse for asking.

"The reason I ask is because some of the teachers' attendance records have my name listed wrong and some of them have been calling me Olive instead of Olivia and I figured that was because the registration forms were screwed up."

This seemed to put her mind at ease, but stupid me had to second-guess myself and keep talking.

"I don't mean some of the teachers called me Olive, I meant to say that all the teachers called me Olive, of course, because my name was wrong on the registration. I meant to say all of them called me Olive on the first day and I corrected them, but some of them still call me Olive just because they forgot what I told them."

Things had been going well but now I could tell that she wasn't buying what I was selling.

"Olivia, is there something you're not telling me about?"

I shook my head and acted as if my mouth was too full of food to speak. She seemed to be considering whether or not she wanted to answer my question.

"Well … I just assumed that your parents were going to register you for classes, but I suppose I'd best check with them on that and see what went wrong."

My mouth was very suddenly not full of food. "Oh, you don't have to do that. I've taken care of it. There are only one or two teachers that forget to call me Olivia, but I'll straighten things out with them first thing tomorrow."

"That sounds good. Why don't you go ahead and straighten things out, and I'll call the school tomorrow afternoon to make certain it's all straight."

I knew from her tone of voice that she was serious about calling the school. That was one major difference between my parents and Aunt Jennifer. When she said she was going to do something, she sure as hell did it.

After dinner, I went out for a stroll. I thought there was something wrong with my eyes, because my vision was very blurry. My skull was filled with cotton candy instead of brain matter. I just sort of wandered around in a daze. My chest was empty and it seemed like the air outside was very thick because I couldn't pull it into my lungs.

I felt the sudden urge to go find a skateboard or a bicycle or something, but after dark all the garage doors were closed so I was out of luck for any of that. I avoided Cecilia's house and walked around the block. Then I started thinking and trying to figure out what I was going to do to keep my aunt from calling the school. I could cut her phone lines, but then she'd just use her cell phone. I could cut her phone lines and hide her cell phone, but she'd probably get wise to a tactic like that and I'd be the first place she'd hunt for a perpetrator. I could hire someone to tie her up, but I didn't have any money and I knew I probably didn't have the guts or the strength to tie her up by myself.

During all this thinking I'd accidentally wandered down Cecilia's street. I found myself standing in front of her house looking at her stupid bedroom window and thinking about how I wouldn't be in this dilemma if it wasn't for her.

I was overcome by a flaming bonfire of anger. The cotton candy inside me was burnt to a crisp by a gasoline-fueled fire.

I grabbed a brick that was being used as edging for her walkway. I picked it up and hurled it at Cecilia's bedroom window. I wasn't thinking when I did it. I know that. But it felt good to do it nonetheless. It felt good until I heard the sound of Cecilia's muted voice. She didn't scream or yell, but instead I simply heard a simple "Ouch" within a second or so after I tossed the brick.

I stood there staring until I saw Cecilia poke her face through her broken window. She was rubbing her head with one hand and I could just barely make out a small scrape on her forehead and a tiny trickle of blood making its way down her nose.

"Olivia?"

I quickly ran and hid behind the big oak that stood in her front yard.

"Olivia? I can see you out there, you know."

For some reason I didn't come out but instead stayed hidden as best I could.

"All right, if you don't want to come out then I guess I'll come down."

Cecilia then moved over to her second bedroom window and lifted it and crawled out onto the small section of roof next to the dormer-style window. She carefully traversed the shingles and then jumped a good five or six feet to a low-hanging branch of the oak. Once on the branch, she lowered herself to the ground beside me. She was still rubbing her head.

"What the heck? You couldn't toss a few pebbles to get my attention?"

I didn't know exactly what to say. All the anger that possessed me when I picked up the brick was mostly gone. I just kinda stared at her.

"Where have you been?" she asked.

I still stared and I guess she could tell that I was still a little bit angry.

"Why are you mad at me? Is that why you threw a brick? Because you're pissed about something?"

"Don't play stupid with me," I told her.

Then, she took her turn at staring and not saying a word.

We both stood there for what seemed like forever, neither of us muttering anything. The scratch on her head was small. Not the kind of thing you'd think a brick would do. It looked more like a little cat scratch.

"Seriously, Olivia, I don't get what you're upset about."

"Listen, I don't need to be friends with you. We were friends for the summer, which is fine. But then I get to school on the first day and you're too busy being an Ambassador and apparently you're embarrassed to be seen with me, so ... whatever."

My last words hung in the air like something that hangs in the air for a very long time. Like smoke, I suppose. Or a helium balloon. Or a couple of tennis shoes dangling from an electrical wire. Or a kite in the wind. Like a ... like a ... thirteen-year-old girl's breathless panting on a cold day.

I waited.

"Olivia, I'm sorry I was so busy being an Ambassador. I'm

not embarrassed by you at all. You're my best friend."

And the crystallized cloud of breathless panting formed into icy dew drops and fell to the snow below. And the kite sailed off over the ocean. And electrical wires sparked and caught fire and the laces turned to ash and the tennis shoes fell to the pavement. And the helium balloon exploded and the smoke drifted into wispy lines and spun like a twister and flew off helter-skelter into the atmosphere.

I smiled.

"You're my best friend too."

CHAPTER 10

We spent the rest of the night scheming about how I'd get out of this mess with school.

We figured it was likely that Mom and Dad simply never bothered to register me for any classes, so we had to figure out a way to get it done. Luck was on our side, though, because Cecilia was a volunteer in the front office (of course) and she had access to all of the forms and passwords and anything we'd need to get the ball rolling. The only problem, though, was that she didn't work the office until fourth period and there was always a chance that my aunt would call before then. That's when Cecilia came up with the idea for forwarding all the calls.

She told me it was as simple as hitting the line you wanted to forward and then punching in *72 followed by 9 and then the area code and number you wanted to forward the call to. At first we thought we would forward the calls to my aunt's house, since she'd be at work. Then we reconsidered because we wouldn't be able to forward them again back to the office. It would seem very strange for the principal and vice principal and all the people in the office if they didn't get any phone calls during the whole day.

We had to think of a phone somewhere within the building itself so that we could answer outside calls and then transfer them back to a number in the front office when the calls were not my aunt.

We considered one of the counselor's offices since one or the other was often out for the day, but if they were all there, that wouldn't work.

We thought about the custodial closet, but figured it probably didn't have a phone line, just an intercom system.

We also tossed the teacher's lounge into the mix, but knew it was unlikely that we could get away with it considering how popular it was for teachers when they had their free periods.

Then, Cecilia came up with the brilliant idea of the nurse's office since the nurse didn't come in until noon. Cecilia said the school district had cut the nurse's position in half and they figured it was better for him to come in during the second half of the day than the first because kids were more likely to be hurt during the afternoon.

When she said "him" about the nurse, I was taken aback. Even though I knew that nurses could be men, I'd never met one, but Cecilia assured me that he was a guy.

As we figured it, Cecilia would have to come up with an excuse to get into the main office for a few short minutes first thing in the morning, to forward the phones and get the keys to the nurse's office. Then she'd sneak me into the nurse's office and I'd handle the phones there until a little before noon. Since the nurse came in at noon, and Cecilia didn't work the office until one, there was a small hole in the plan. But we figured that out too.

Cecilia would drop by the office one more time before lunch and forward the phones to a telephone on which she had turned off the ringer. Then there would be about that hour during which the un-ringered phone would get all the calls, but she would set it up with a voicemail that said something like, "Sorry, the whole office is out to lunch." We figured we could get away with that for one short hour and the ladies in the office wouldn't miss the fact that they weren't getting any calls.

Then, during fourth period, Cecilia would show up at the main office and keep the phones forwarded just long enough to get on the computer and add me to the list of registered students and get me some good classes. As soon as she finished, I could go to class and introduce myself to the teacher and tell her that I was new.

By the time Aunt Jennifer called, everything would be kosher.

I didn't sleep well that night before we tried our plan. I snuck into the house a little late, and then I lay there in bed and stared straight up into the air. The spray-on, popcorn-textured ceiling began to flow like trippy rivers of white oatmeal floating in white lava. I lay there and thought about Mom and Dad. I didn't really care what they thought about anything, mostly because they didn't care whether or not I cared. Then I thought about my aunt and I wondered why I did care what she thought. Then I thought about Cecilia and the strange thing about her was that she didn't seem to care, but then again, in some ways she cared more than others.

The thing with Cecilia was that in some ways she cared more than anyone, but the way she cared was different. Most people cared and they made it your fault that they cared so much. Cecilia cared, but seemed to understand that her caring was all her own crap and nobody else's fault.

At some point I must have fallen asleep, because at some other point I woke up.

Cecilia and I agreed to meet down the block from my house so my aunt wouldn't get too suspicious. After all, Cecilia and I hadn't been walking together to school lately. I told Aunt Jennifer that I had to be at school early that day because I was going to try out for chorus and that's when they held their tryouts. Cecilia and I got to the school about forty-five minutes before any of the other kids arrived.

"Just act like you're normal and you belong here. Nobody will question it."

"What if someone asks who I am?"

"They won't. The only way they'll ask you who you are is if you're some scuzzy-looking guy that looks like you're up to no good. They're not going to question a kid."

We arrived at the school and Cecilia said hi to some of the teachers that we saw in the halls. I cracked a fake smile, but I couldn't bring myself to smile for real 'cause I was too nervous. She led me to her locker, which was conveniently located between the main office and the nurse's office. Cecilia gave me her locker combo and told me to just mess around with the stuff in her locker and pretend like it was mine while I waited. Then she disappeared behind the main office door.

Cecilia's locker was neat and organized. On the inside of the door, she'd taped her Ambassador nametag along with three pictures. One was of a bald guy with glasses who had a Bluetooth headset in his ear and some sort of orange robe on. I didn't know it at the time, but it was a picture of the Dalai Lama. The other photo was harder to make out. It was a black and white picture from probably the '70s or so. At first, I couldn't make out what was going on, but it looked to be another Buddhist-monk-looking guy.

This one was sitting on the sidewalk engulfed in flames.

There was a white canister next to him and an antique car in the background with the hood open. I wasn't sure if this was supposed to be some sort of performance art, or magic trick or what, but something about the picture made me feel uncomfortable.

The third picture was another bald person, but this was not a monk. This picture was of a bald woman with an uneasy smile. Her eyes looked tired and you could tell that she was trying very hard to put on an air of comfort and happiness, but she had very little life left in her.

This was obviously Cecilia's mom.

I looked at the photos for a long time. It seemed to take Cecilia forever to get the phones forwarded and come out with the keys to the nurse's office. A couple of teachers walked by, and I buried my head half into the locker and acted like I was supposed to be there, but I knew that I didn't. I knew I looked like I didn't belong, because I never looked like I belonged. Usually I was decent at faking it, but not this time. I tried my damnedest to fake like I fit in here in this town, in this school at this locker. But I'm pretty sure I looked like I fit in about as much as those flames looked like they fit in around that monk. About as much as that crooked smile looked like it belonged on the face of Cecilia's mom.

I sat there buried in Cecilia's thin locker, my face filled with self-pity and self-loathing.

Cecilia emerged from the office and jangled the keys in front of her. The smile on her face was genuine and I realized at that moment that her smile was always genuine. I think Cecilia always felt like she belonged.

"Let's go," she said in a soft voice.

We both looked up and down the hall before sliding the key into the door of the nurse's office, then sliding ourselves into the darkness.

"Don't turn the light on or you'll attract attention," I said.

This time I turned my lips up into a genuine smile. I'd always been very good at remaining undetected while sneaking around.

"I'll try a test call in a couple minutes," she told me as she left me alone in the nurse's office.

After Cecilia's test call, the lines got busy for awhile. Most of the calls were obviously parents calling in sick for their kids. I would cut them off quickly and then transfer them to the open line Cecilia told me to use in the main office. Some of the "parents" calling in sick for their kids sounded pretty dang young, which cracked my butt up. I got the impression that this school was going to be just fine for me. That is, if the ladies in the office were buying what some of these young voices were selling.

After the first class bell rang, the phone calls slowed way down, so I had a little time to snoop around in the nurse's desk. In the top drawer, he had a little divider thing filled with paper clips and pens and one of the cups even had a ton of change in it. I removed a few bucks' worth of quarters and put them in my pocket. I didn't want to take so much that he'd notice them missing, and I dug through the remaining change to bring more quarters up from the bottom of the pile. Less likely he'd miss anything that way.

The next drawer down had a bunch of files with names on them. I looked for "Cecilia French," but didn't find a file, which I figure meant that she had never been sick. I didn't know any of the other names, so I didn't bother trying to look anything up on any of them.

The third drawer had a bunch of tablets of forms and such, which didn't interest me, so I got up from the desk and started looking around the room. The medicine cabinet was securely locked. To get in that thing, a person would need some heavy-duty safecracking equipment and some expertise that I didn't have.

I was in the process of opening the cabinet door under the sink when I heard a noise that caused me first to jump and then to freeze. It was the sound of a man's voice talking to someone down the hall while opening the door to the nurse's office. He half-continued the conversation as the door swung wide and left me trapped there.

He looked right at me curiously, but continued talking to the disembodied voice down the hall so as to not give me up. He shut the door behind him and then looked at me with a crap-eating grin.

"Well, well. What do we have here?"

CHAPTER 11

The guy's name was Nurse Joe. And Nurse Joe turned out to be a Class A asswipe. Nurse Joe was the kind of guy who started out all nice and smiling and made a person think that he was some sort of friendly character.

"Is somebody trying to avoid third period?" He asked me. "Don't worry. I'm not out to get anyone in trouble. If you need a place to hide out for a bit, we can just sit you down on one of the cots and we'll write it up that you're having some sort of female problems."

And then he gave me this cheesy, horrible grin that told me I better watch out. It told me that Old Joe had something up his sleeve and he wasn't going to do any giving unless he did some taking too. And no, I don't mean in any sort of pervy way. In fact, I thought that Nurse Joe was probably gay or something because I never got a pervy-interested-in-young-girls vibe off the guy. But believe me when I tell you that creeper grownups sometimes have more ideas up their sleeves besides pervy things.

"Go ahead and lay yourself down here on the cot and I'll give you a little something to help the pain go away."

I didn't fight with the guy about it all. I just took the pill he gave me, which I pretty much recognized as an aspirin, and I tossed the pill in the little wastebasket when his back was turned. He started a chart for me and told me that I could hang out in here for a while if I wanted.

Then he went back to his desk and I sat there crossing my fingers and hoping that the phone didn't ring. Which, of course, it did.

"Nurse's office." He answered and then paused. "No, I'm

sorry. But I can transfer you. Just a moment."

I sat there awhile longer and again crossed my fingers and hoped the phone wouldn't ring, but it rang right away again. I knew I had another forty-five minutes or so before Cecilia would transfer the phones to voicemail, and the way I figured it, Nurse Joe had another two or three transfers before he'd get wise to the fact that something funny was going on with the phone system.

"Nurse's office … Oh that's strange … I thought I transferred you to the main office but it just came back here. What number did you originally call? … Hmm … no. Let me go see what's going on. Give me five minutes and then try calling that number again."

Then he stood and smiled at me as he began walking toward the door. "I'll be right back."

I could feel my heart pound against my shirt.

"Hold on a minute, Nurse Joe."

"What's the problem, Olivia?"

"I don't exactly have a problem, but I have a proposition for you."

He let the door shut and stepped back inside. The minute he did that, I knew that I was right about him being some sort of scheming, up-to-no-good kind of a guy. In fact, he raised one eyebrow exactly like a scheming, up-to-no-good kind of a guy would do when offered a proposition.

"What's this proposition all about?"

"Well, here's what I'm thinking. I'm thinking that I guy like you could maybe use the help of a girl like me."

"Oh, and what exactly do you mean by that, little Miss Thing?" And he did say that as if he were some sort of a perv, though I knew in my gut that he wasn't, and I have a pretty good gut for things like that.

"Here's the thing…." I hesitated. I'd have to keep my offer of help as something generic as opposed to specific. I'd have to keep it general enough that he saw the value in keeping me around and keeping on my good side.

"My idea is that…"

Then the phone rang again and he stepped over to his desk to answer it. This gave me a few more seconds to consider my proposal.

"Nurse's office … No, I'm sorry. I think there is something screwy with the phone tree right now. I'm about to check into it. If you could call back in five minutes, I should have it sorted out by then."

He began to walk toward me, but then walked past and continued on toward the door. "I'll be back in a minute and we can discuss your proposal."

And he was out the door before I had a chance to stop him.

I was up off that cot as fast as a … as fast as a … as fast as a girl who is about to get in trouble by a creepy male nurse at a school she doesn't even belong in. I knew I had to stop him before he got to the front office and got that phone forwarding fixed.

Though I thought of myself as quick, when I burst through the door and hit the hallway, he was already entering the front office. I came up on the main office door, but didn't enter because I heard him speaking to one of the office ladies.

"I think there's something screwed up with the phone tree because all of your calls are being forwarded to my office."

I didn't stick around to hear any more about it.

In retrospect, the nice thing to do would have been to leave a note on Cecilia's locker or something, but I felt a deep need to get the hell out of there. I ran through the front door of the school and ran down the steps and didn't look back until I was at Merle Hay Mall at the little deli downstairs in the food court playing vintage video games. I was in a zone and don't even remember if I played Centipede or Dig-Dug that day. They also had Joust, but I do remember that some other kid who was obviously skipping school was hogging that machine.

I remember that because I kept looking over at him while he was concentrating. And out of the corner of my eye, I caught him looking over at me while I was concentrating too. He was older than me. Maybe tenth grade. He was a black kid with short, scraggly dreds and he had his lower lip pierced and I remember thinking that I couldn't believe a kid who was so young would have parents who would let him get his lip pierced.

We both played our games and took turns looking over at one

another. Then, at some point, I saw him out of the corner of my eyes and he left his game and wandered over to stand a few feet behind me. At first, I was able to ignore him, but it kept throwing my concentration off and it also annoyed the crap out of me. I kept getting killed, so I finally turned to him right before my last life got taken.

"You're annoying the crap out of me. Would you mind standing somewhere else while you wait for this game?"

He shrugged and walked back over to stand in front of Joust, but instead of playing the game himself, he leaned on the machine and kept staring right at me. This pissed me off even more, and I immediately got killed this time. I turned and marched at the smug little jerk and got right up in his face.

"What the hell is your problem? Can't you leave me alone while you're waiting to play?"

He smiled confidently and made it obvious he wasn't scared of me, but also made it seem like he was truly apologetic for causing me any trouble.

"I wasn't waiting to play the game. I was just trying to figure out who you are. Shouldn't you be in school?"

"Shouldn't you be in school?"

"Nah. I already graduated. I'm taking a quarter off because I got a late acceptance into college. I start winter quarter."

"College? There's no way you're old enough for college."

"I was homeschooled so I got a little ahead of things."

"How old are you?"

"I'm fifteen, but my parents pulled me out of elementary school in fifth grade because they're freaks like that. My dad is a psychologist and my mom is a yoga instructor." He added the last part after a pause as if it was supposed to explain everything.

I stared at him to try and get a line on this kid. You'd think with a story like that he was full of it. But he seemed very sincere.

"What college are you going to?"

"Julliard," he answered. Then he added, "It's a music school. I'm a musician."

I felt a bit pissed again that he was treating me like some sort of idiot. Like I didn't know what Julliard was. But I held myself back and tried to think, What Would Cecilia Do? That was a little game I'd been playing with myself lately. Kinda like that whole thing, What Would Jesus Do? I imagined that I was Cecilia and tried to be nice and not reactionary like I usually was. Cecilia seemed the opposite of reactionary, so I figured her to be a good model on that count.

"What do you do?" he asked.

"What do I do? I'm a kid. I don't do anything yet."

"I mean what do you want to do with your life in order to make a difference in the world?"

I shrugged, but made my brain again ask WWCD.

"What instrument do you play?" I asked, practically hearing the words the way they would have come out of Cecilia's mouth all dripping with sincerity and interest.

"A little of everything. Guitar, violin, bass, piano, drums. I can play woodwinds all right, but they're not my favorite. A little trumpet. A little trombone."

"Jesus! What are you? Some sort of a child prodigy?"

The kid laughed. "Nah. My dad's very interested in music, so I learned a lot from him."

I shrugged and grinned.

The pause after the laugh caught me off guard and I started to feel a little pissed about something again. I felt my eyebrows furrowing into a V-shape and I didn't mean to do it, but the blood in my body seemed to move up into my forehead and scrunch it up that way.

Before I said something stupid, though, the kid smiled again and reached out his hand, and I jumped back a little bit because I thought he was going to grab me or something. Instead he kept his hand there, waiting for a handshake, and introduced himself.

"My name's Ian."

I shook hands and for some reason—to this day I don't know why I did it—I introduced myself and it didn't come out the way I'd planned on saying it.

"My name's Cecilia." I lied.

"It's very nice to meet you, Cecilia. Want to go two-player on this machine?"

I nodded and I stood next to him and pretended to be Cecilia. My arm occasionally brushed his arm and I could feel my breath getting a little shallow standing so close to Ian. I could feel my heart beating fast too, but in a good way. And I knew that I was in big trouble now because I had just fallen in love.

CHAPTER 12

Before he left the deli, Ian asked me for my phone number and I gave it to him. My aunt's phone number actually, because I didn't have my own phone yet.

I was late getting home, but I walked slowly anyway because I was nervous. Who knew what my aunt had figured out about me skipping school? I thought about stopping by Cecilia's house to find out how it all went, but as far as I knew, she was toast and had gotten busted for the whole thing. I didn't want to face her under these circumstances. Plus, the whole thing made me feel really weird with Ian and the fact that I pretended to be Cecilia. And I still didn't understand why I did that. Why didn't I just say my name is Olivia?

When I arrived home, my aunt treated me no different than she ever did.

"How was school today?"

"Good."

"Did you do anything special? Anything different happen today?"

"Nope."

I couldn't tell if she was trying to catch me in something or not. She started dinner and I set the table. It had become our routine to do this every night, and I honestly couldn't remember how or when she got me to start setting the table. I remembered that she used to try and get me to set the table when my parents first moved to their place. I would argue about it and tell her that I wasn't going to eat in that case. But somehow, somewhere along the line, I started doing it.

"I'm excited to meet your teachers at the Parent Teacher

conference next week."

"You're going?" I asked and I feel like I did a decent job of acting as if I already knew about the conference.

"Sure. I want to talk to them and hear about how you're doing."

I felt stiff in the back of my neck when she said this and I turned my head from one way to the other until I felt a sort of crack and listened for the cracking sound. Only, you know how sometimes cracking your neck like that makes you feel all relaxed and other times, there is this shooting pain that burns its way up from your shoulder and it feels like your neck is suddenly on fire. And there is no satisfying crack sound, just the burning and … and … damn if I was going to let my damn aunt come to a parent-teacher conference when she was not my parent and she was not my teacher and while I was thinking all this I was getting more and more pissed and I was pretty much sick and tired of her acting like she was my parent. For that matter, she wasn't a parent at all. She was obviously too screwed up of a person to even find another person to get together with, let alone have kids with, and now I was suffering for it.

I was like a little doll that she thought she could make do whatever she wanted me to do and the fact was that I was no doll and I sure as hell was not going to be her goddamn doll. Stupid bitch. I worked my ass off and this was what I got? I put up with my ridiculous and embarrassing parents and I put up with setting her goddamn table even though I never asked to live here with her. I never asked to have to live with all of her shitty rules and her ridiculous things like her arbitrary questions and all the bullshit she put me through. I never asked to be born and I sure as hell never asked to be born into this messed-up family where the people who were supposed to care didn't give a shit and some stranger cares so much that she stomps all over my civil rights.

What happened next seemed like it was happening to someone else. I felt as if I floated above the kitchen and watched it.

I took the big heavy plate that was in my right hand and I flung it like a Frisbee at my aunt's head, and I saw it strike the back of her skull.

She turned to me as if clock hands were moving at the speed of ketchup. She turned to me with a funny look on her face as if she had no idea what had happened. She looked all surprised, and then her face turned a bit green, and her eyes rolled into the back of her head and she dropped to the ground. The back of her head, the same one that I'd just hit with a plate, bounced off the kitchen counter before she landed.

"Holy shit! I just killed my aunt!" I yelled to nobody in particular.

I ran to the phone and called Cecilia. "Holy shit! I just killed my aunt!"

"What?"

"I killed Aunt Jennifer!"

"Calm down, Olivia. What do you mean that you killed your aunt?"

"Just what I said. I killed her with a Frisbee. I mean a plate. I killed her with a plate that I threw at her like it was a Frisbee."

"Are you sure she's dead?"

"Yes, of course. She fell to the floor and she ... she...." I noticed that her chest was moving up and down with her breath. "Wait. She may still be alive. She's breathing."

"Hang up and call 911," Cecilia told me.

"But ... I ... they'll arrest me."

"Just do it. Better to be arrested for assault than murder. Call 911 and tell them that your aunt fell. Then get rid of the evidence and wait for the ambulance. I'm coming right over."

I did what Cecilia told me, but it wasn't as simple as she made it sound. The emergency operator made me stay on the line and she asked me all kinds of questions about the way my aunt was breathing and how much she was breathing, and on and on, so that I couldn't pick up all the broken pieces of plate. And then, before I even got off the phone, I heard the paramedics at the front door and the 911 lady told me to go unlock it and let them in, which I did.

And then they asked me some questions and started to check her out with stethoscopes and blood pressure cuffs and my aunt started to come awake some while they were doing it. They asked me what she hit her head on when she fainted and I didn't bother to correct them about the fainting. I pointed to the counter and there was a little blood and hair on the corner, so they seemed to believe me. Nobody even asked me about the broken plate. I suppose they figured my aunt just dropped it when she fell.

Then I heard more footsteps toward the front of the house, and I knew I was in trouble because it was probably the cops, though it turned out to be Cecilia. They put Aunt Jennifer on a stretcher and let me ride in the front passenger seat of the ambulance because I was a kid and couldn't drive myself there. Cecilia was told that she'd have to get a ride from her dad, though.

Throughout all of this, I kept expecting the police to show up, but they never did.

Then, while Cecilia and her dad and I sat in the waiting room, I kept expecting the cops again, but still no cops.

Finally, a doctor came out and basically told us that everything was all right, but anytime a person goes unconscious like that, even for a short time, it's best to run an MRI and also keep them overnight for observation. He told us that we could go in and visit her now, so we did.

The walk down the hospital hallway was like a walk from my death row cell to the executioner's room. I felt like I had shackles on my ankles. I felt like Mr. French was my lawyer and Cecilia was my priest and they were taking me to the chair.

The hospital smelled like rubbing alcohol. I've heard before that hospitals smell like death, but this one just smelled super sterile. There were people walking down the hall very slowly dragging IV bags on little wheeled towers. There was a lady pushing her vegetable of a husband in a wheelchair. His head was facing the ground like he had no muscles at all in his neck, but she smiled at us when we came upon her.

"You've got a couple cute ones there," she said to Mr. French.

"I'm not his," I told her. "He's just my friend's dad."

She smiled like she understood why I wanted to distance myself, but then shot a look to Mr. French that more or less said Boy, isn't she a touchy little bitch.

I shot her a dirty look.

A couple of nurses passed us by and they smiled at us too. Maybe they were trying to help me feel better. I realized that none of these smiling people probably had any idea who my aunt was. They just saw this girl walking down the hall with a look on her face like she was about to keel over. They probably figured that my mom or dad just died or something. As far as they knew, I was some sort of cancer patient with only a few weeks left to live. I'm pretty sure that's what my face looked like.

Then, as we closed in on Aunt Jennifer's room, I got a slight break. Mom and Dad came out of the elevator.

"Olivia. Are you all right?"

I just broke down in tears and Mom stood back like she didn't know what to do. Dad came over and put his big hairy arm around my shoulders and then squatted down and gave me a huge hug like the kind of thing he might have done when I was a little kid.

"There, there, pumpkin. What happened to Aunt Jennifer?"

I could smell the whiskey and beer on his breath, but it didn't make me feel mad like you'd probably expect. It more made me feel comfortable, like I was part of a family again. Smelling the whiskey made me want to hug Dad even harder. Unlike my aunt, Dad actually needed me. My aunt ran around acting like I needed her, but my parents were the opposite and that felt comforting.

"It's okay. What happened, sweetie?"

At that moment, I knew that I was going to spill the beans about everything. I was going to tell Mom and Dad about skipping school and about stealing stuff and about that creep Nurse Joe and about hitting Aunt Jennifer upside the head with a plate. And I figured that the minute they heard it all, Dad would be pissed for a minute, but then he'd hug me even tighter and realize that he had to get me out of the situation with Aunt Jennifer. Maybe we'd need to move to a whole new town again, or maybe they'd let me sleep in the bathtub in their studio apartment.

"How did your Aunt Jennifer get hurt?" he asked.

Before I could say a word, Aunt Jennifer walked out of her room.

"There's my little hero," she said to me. "You may have saved my life with your quick thinking."

Cecilia and I looked at one another, and then back at my aunt, who was in a hospital gown and dragging one of those IV towers alongside her.

"What in the world happened, Jenn?" My dad asked.

"I'm honestly not sure. You know how sometimes you get a little crook in your neck and you twist your neck to try and snap it loose?"

We all nodded our heads.

"It was like I got one of those crooks in my neck, only instead of a little crook it was like this big thump of a pain and it shot down from my skull and down my neck into my shoulder and then I remember hearing a dish break—I was doing dishes. And then I looked at Olivia and simply fell over and fainted. They tell me I cracked my head pretty good on the kitchen counter. Then, this little hero daughter of yours called 911 and saved me."

Everyone all slapped me on the back and smiled and laughed and you'd think that in a situation like that, knowing what I knew, I'd have felt totally uncomfortable and pained and embarrassed because I wasn't any sort of hero. But I'll tell you the truth: I was smiling and laughing right along with them, because I did feel like a hero. I really did call the ambulance. I truly did help to save my aunt.

We all spoke at once about what it was like in the ambulance and how my parents got the call from Mr. French and we were all very excited and my dad said, "Maybe I should call my friend Chet Fergusson over at Channel 5 News about our hero here."

I was standing there wondering how in the hell my dad had a friend over at Channel 5 news, but then I remembered all the Freedom and Liberty Party crap he'd been up to. Everyone else seemed to be thinking about me: the hero.

The nurse next to my aunt was smiling. Even Mom had a big ol' grin on her face. Even Mr. French.

But when I turned to look at Cecilia, she was definitely not smiling.

CHAPTER 13

My aunt stayed the night in the hospital for observation and I said goodbye to Cecilia and her dad, and I got in the car with my parents and we started driving back toward Urbandale. We drove in silence when all hell broke loose because Dad turned left instead of going straight.

"WHERE ARE YOU GOING?" Mom yelled at him.

She almost never yelled like that. Let me rephrase that: she yelled like that maybe three times in the whole time I knew her. I don't remember the other circumstances, but I would never forget what she sounded like when she was all hysterical like that. Unlike Dad and me, when Mom got all crazy pissed, her eyes opened up wide. Dad and I squinted when we were pissed off. But Mom opened her eyes wide, and yelled it again in this horrible shriek as she pounded on the dashboard.

"WHERE THE HELL ARE YOU GOING?"

Dad stayed pretty calm considering, and it made me wonder if maybe he wasn't used to her yelling like that. Maybe she'd been yelling like that a lot while I'd been staying with my aunt. Maybe she'd yelled a lot like that before I was even born.

"What do you mean, where am I going? I'm taking Olivia back to Jennifer's house."

"No you're not," Mom said.

"What do you mean I'm not?"

"She just found Jennifer all passed out and looking like she was dead. Don't you even realize how traumatic that must be for her?"

"I didn't really think about it."

"We're not just going to drop her off, Reggie, like an ashtray full of your cigarette butts on the side of the road. Olivia needs to be with her parents right now."

My dad didn't answer, but he turned right the next time he could and began heading toward their apartment.

"She can sleep in the bed with me and you can sleep on the sofa."

Again, Dad said nothing.

"You pass out there half the time anyway."

The rest of the drive was silent.

I sat in the back seat and couldn't shake the grin that curled up the corners of my lips. I don't know if I thought it was funny that Mom acted like that or maybe I thought it was funny that Dad just took it. Maybe I just thought it was funny how they had the whole conversation as if I wasn't even there listening to the whole thing.

Whatever it was, I was still grinning when I got to their apartment and cuddled up in bed next to Mom, and heard Dad sawing logs in the living room.

Whatever had me smiling that night, though, was gone by the next day. I awoke and found Mom and Dad gone. Taped to the front door with a Band-Aid was a hastily scribbled note written on a paper towel.

Gone to the hospital. We'll call you when we find out more.

What the hell?

I freaked out. Find out more. What does that mean? Find out more?

Something had obviously gone wrong with my aunt.

My first instinct was to call Cecilia, but I felt anxious about it since she seemed pissed at me last night at the hospital. So, instead, I tossed on one of Mom's jackets and I rushed out the door and walked to the closest bus stop that I knew about. That took about an hour since Urbandale is not real big on buses. Then, I had practically another hour to wait because it was the weekend and they don't run very often.

Standing at the bus stop, I had nothing better to do then read what I could of the Des Moines Register through the little window of the newspaper box. The story on top was about the big Freedom and Liberty Party rally that was coming up and right there in the fifth paragraph there was a quote from Dad. My very own dad really was becoming famous.

"… according to FLP spokesperson Reggie Driscoll, "We are excited to see how welcoming the""

And the article stopped there because the rest of it was on the other side of the fold of the paper. I reached in my pocket for change to by a copy, but I didn't have any change because I'd totally spaced out on bringing any money, which also didn't bode well for catching the bus.

I looked around for a rock so I could bust out the newspaper box window and just as I found one and was about to commit a misdemeanor, the bus rolled up and I had to hop on. I gave the driver a sob story about my aunt, and the note my parents left me and everything. She was understanding and let me ride for free.

Then, the ride itself took what seemed like forever, which gave me a lot of time to think. Mostly I was thinking about why Cecilia was pissed at me, but I was also thinking about hitting my aunt in the head and also thinking I was totally screwed and would probably be sent to juvie. Especially if she died or something.

As for Cecilia being pissed, I was pissed back at her. Once again she was being a judgmental little jerk because I didn't tell everyone the whole story about what happened with my aunt. But what good would it have done? My aunt was already hurt and all of the admissions and owning up to crap in the world would not help with that.

I also think Cecilia was probably pretty jealous because I was getting all of this attention and she was left in the background. One thing I knew about Cecilia is that she liked being Miss Goody Two-Shoes and she liked being the center of attention. Here they all were talking about putting me on the news and such and she was being relegated to being a nobody like I usually was and she couldn't stand it.

Too bad. So sad.

Just because she was Miss Thing and everyone loved her so much, she couldn't stand for anyone else to be recognized for something good for a change.

Now, this part may be a bit of a surprise after all I just said and all I went through to get to the hospital. But when I got there,

I couldn't bring myself to go inside.

At first it was because there was a TV van sitting out front and my heart started pumping a million beats a minute and I was afraid they were either there to do a story about me being a hero or they were going to do a story about me being a murderer. Either way, I didn't much feel like being interviewed.

But then, the TV van drove away and I realized they probably weren't there about anything to do with me anyway. Still, my heart was beating too fast and I couldn't deal with going inside and facing up to Mom and Dad and the doctors and whatever was happening with my aunt.

At the same time, I didn't feel like talking my way onto another bus and riding all the way back to Mom and Dad's little apartment, so I just started walking.

Mercy Hospital was clear on the far side of Des Moines, and I didn't have a great sense of space or time, but I pretty much figured that I wouldn't be getting all the way to Urbandale by walking. So I started walking the opposite direction. I'd never been in that part of town and it definitely seemed sketchy and I felt like the people were all staring at me like I didn't belong. And it wasn't just because most of the folks on the street were black people and Mexican people. There were some white people too, and nobody looked at them the way they looked at me.

I think they looked at me differently because they knew.

I don't have any idea how they knew, but I think they knew that I was a murderer now. I think they knew what I had done and I was now in a different league than everyone else. I was officially a bad person. I had flirted with the idea of being a bad person for many years now, but when I picked up that plate and threw it, it all became totally official and I crossed the line.

My thoughts were interrupted when some guy whistled to me out his car window: "Hey! You looking for a party?"

I just rolled my eyes and shrugged my shoulders and looked the other way, but he pulled up on me and leaned across the seat and tried to talk to me again.

"You know where a party is?" he asked.

This time he sounded even more like an idiot. He had just acted like he knew where a party was and now he was acting like he didn't and I should know. Of course, I realized the party he was talking about was in his pants, but it still irked me when someone came across as such a numbnutz even when they were trying to pick up a thirteen-year-old girl on the street.

Rather than answer, I continued to ignore him and kept walking, but then I realized that he had probably just mistaken me for a hooker since I was wearing my Mom's long jacket and my shorts underneath.

After I thought of that, I figured I should set the record straight. "Sorry, you're barking up the wrong whore, buddy. I'm just a girl out for a walk with a can of Mace and 9-1-1 on speed dial."

He pulled the car in front of me at the next driveway as if he were going to try something, but instead he reached into the collar of his shirt and removed a little leather holder with a badge on a chain.

CHAPTER 14

"No need to call 9-1-1, missy. I've got your 9-1-1 right here. What I want to know from you is what you're doing walking around this neighborhood in that outfit."

"I'm just ... I am...."

Now, I'm not usually short on having anything to say, but the deal is that the guy took my by a pretty big surprise. I was expecting a perv and not a cop, though I also realize they are sometimes one and the same. But the point is that I had my perv replies ready and not my cop replies.

So, because of my little hiccup, I had to try and remember how to deal with cops. Let's see ... for an ex-military cop, let the tears flow. For a nerdy, ugly cop, call him a perv. For a nice, friendly cop, be nice. Only problem was that the cop there in front of me who was motioning for me to come toward him didn't seem to fit any of the profiles. He was too scraggly-looking to be ex-military. He was too good-looking and confident to be a nerd. And the frown on his face was anything but friendly.

"I know you don't live around here. So again, I'm going to ask you, what are you doing in this neighborhood?"

"I just ... I just got back from the hospital and I didn't have any bus fare so I'm walking home."

"This is not a very good neighborhood to walk in. Where do you live?"

"Urbandale."

"Well, if you came from Mercy Hospital, you're walking the wrong way."

"I guess I got twisted around." I answered, though I knew the minute it came out of my mouth it didn't sounding convincing. One thing about being a good liar is that you also know when you're not pulling it off.

The cop pulled some cell phone/walkie-talkie thing from under his seat and called for some sort of backup. I didn't understand everything he said, but I caught the word female in the middle of all the blabbering.

Within a few seconds, an old clunker car pulled up alongside the curb and a lady got out of the driver's seat and pulled a badge from her pocket and clipped it on her belt. She kept both eyes on me as she walked to the driver's side of her partner's car and they spoke in hushed tones. Then she walked around the car and approached me.

"We're on the lookout for drug dealers and users here in this neighborhood," she said. "Will you consent to a search so I can see if you're carrying any drugs?"

Now, I learned from a couple of hip-hop songs that you should never consent to a search, and I'm not one to simply roll over and do whatever a cop or anybody else asks of me, but I was frankly pretty tired. Just plain old tired. Even though I slept like a hibernating bear last night, all this crap was getting to me. Crap up to my eyeballs with my parents and my aunt and school and now some guy cop calling me a whore and now some woman cop who apparently wants to start searching for drugs in my body orifices.

"I'm not consenting to any sort of cavity search." I said emphatically, but the lady cop took me by the arm and led me over to the car and pushed me against it anyway. Admittedly, I'd been crying a lot around this time, but usually I'm a pretty tough broad, as the old folks say. Still, when you think that some strange woman with a gun is about to pull down your pants and spread your butt cheeks apart, even the toughest broad can have a crying fit.

I began to sob. I cried and the guy cop came over to the passenger side of the car because he must have felt bad for me or something. And the lady cop seemed to put on hold her plans of spreading apart my butt cheeks. And I sat there sobbing and the cops shuffled uncomfortably and mostly didn't say anything.

Eventually, my sobs turned into tiny little hiccups and the lady cop asked me where my home was.

I don't know why, but I gave her Cecilia's address.

She went back to her undercover car and made a call on the radio and then came back and said something in a very low voice to the guy cop. She then approached me.

"Darling...."

I absolutely hated to be called "darling" or "sweetie" or "honey." Even when we lived in the South where people said that kind of crap all the time, I cringed every time I heard it.

"Darling ... we're going to take you home."

I nodded when they said it and started sobbing again, though this time I'm pretty sure I was mostly faking it. You know how sometimes you can't tell if you're crying for real or not? Anyway, that's how it was the second time I started crying. I think I was faking it, but then again you never know.

So they both got into the front seat of the lady cop's car with me in the back and they drove me toward home until they were no longer driving me toward home, but instead toward Cecilia's home. When we pulled up in front, the guy cop told me to wait while he headed up toward the front door of Cecilia's house. I watched as Cecilia opened the door and said some things to him and he said some things back. Then he looked around behind him and looked at me and she looked over at me and then they said more things and nodded their heads some and shook their heads some. Since head-shaking was the last thing Cecilia did before the guy cop turned around and headed back to the car, it seemed my chances of this working were low.

But when the cop returned and opened the door, he let me out.

"Your sister explained things to me. Please listen to what she has to say. That one seems to have a good head on her shoulders."

I slowly walked toward Cecilia's house. I kept walking that direction until I heard the door of the cruiser close behind me and the engine rev up and the car leave. I was about twenty feet away from Cecilia when I could tell that the cop car was out of sight.

So I turned away from Cecilia's gaze and hightailed it toward my aunt's house.

Cecilia didn't bother to follow.

When I arrived, I checked around front for a rock under a spare key might be hidden, but I had no luck. I walked around to the back and dug my fingernails in under one of the bricks that lined the path to the garden. I threw it through the back door window and then reached through and unlocked the door.

The blue house was especially quiet. Although it was the middle of the day, the light hit all the blue and made it feel like the gloaming – that time of day after the sun sets, but before it's totally dark. I wandered around the house aimlessly for a while, then went into my aunt's bedroom.

Her bed was made, as it always was.

Even though I'd passed by the room dozens of times, I'd never entered. It felt ... well ... it felt a little strange. Almost felt as if it were a dead person's room. For all I knew, it was a dead person's room.

I walked over to the blue nightstand with the frilly lace doilies that decorated the top. I opened the drawer. There was a small pile of stuff inside: a can of Mace, a notepad and some pens, a copy of the Bible, a copy of a steamy romance novel called The Personal Touch, by Lori Borrill. I dug around a little deeper, but didn't find much else. Stuck in a corner there was a single ear plug. Probably part of a pair from sometime when Aunt Jennifer had trouble sleeping.

Next, I went to her closet, and the minute I walked into it, I could smell my aunt. It smelled like some flowery perfume that she was always wearing. I don't know what kind it was, 'cause I'm not much of a perfume girl. I thumbed along hanger after hanger of blue sweaters and blouses and dresses. I ducked my head under those and saw a dozen or so shoes. On the shelf above the clothes, I found a hat box that held some wigs and a wig box that held a hat.

I thought I heard a noise from downstairs so I snuck away from the closet and stepped past the bedroom door to listen. Turned out to be the sound of wind knocking something about on the porch. Maybe the screen door. It wasn't a person, because it was too rhythmic. But I considered that maybe ghosts were rhythmic too.

I went back into Aunt Jennifer's room and started in again with the top drawer of her dresser. She had a few things that were frillier than I would have expected her to wear. There was also a tiny jewelry box that had mostly cheap costume jewels. I guess I expected to find some sort of sex thing or something—a dirty book or some sort of device for sex or something. I don't know why. But Aunt Jennifer apparently had no dark secrets.

The next few drawers were more of the same: clothes.

The bottom drawer, however, was hard to open. The minute I began to pull on the handles I could tell it was filled with some heavy stuff. Maybe this was where she kept her sex books. Maybe she had a whole drawer full of them.

Instead, though, I discovered newspapers and magazines. Stuff like The New York Times and stuff in foreign languages. Rolling Stone, Harper's … all of them were intact, but they all had bookmarks at different places. I opened the first one and saw some boring story about a protest at someplace called School of the Americas. I skimmed the article that told about a bunch of hippies protesting against war or soldiers or something and they all got arrested.

More bookmarks and more of the same stuff. Stories about protests and stories about riots and stories about anarchists and stories about arsons at new housing developments.

I mostly skimmed the text and didn't understand why my aunt was so interested in these kinds of things.

But then, in an article in the Economist, it all became clear.

The article was about another protest—this one at something called the G8 summit in London. Next to the article, a picture told all the million words, or whatever it is they say pictures tell. The picture was obviously a photo of Aunt Jennifer, only she was twenty years younger or something and she was wearing a nun outfit—you know, a habit with a white collar thing and all. Only her face was totally painted up with blue face paint. She almost looked like some sort of scary clown.

She had huge tears painted under her eyes and her mouth was open in anger as if she were screaming at someone or another.

The caption filled in the blanks: The Blue Nun encounters police resistance at the G8 Summit. Though she won't give her real name, Blue Nun is widely known in anarchist circles. She claims to be blue because her fiancé died in battle in the Middle East when he threw himself atop a grenade to save a group of local children.

As you might imagine, I was like: Holy shit.

I think I may have even said it aloud.

I looked back over the articles I'd skimmed and found references to and quotes from the Blue Nun.

She was a celebrity.

I dug deeper and found a couple of old high school yearbooks with her picture inside. The one from her senior year also had a picture of Dad in there when he was a freshman.

I pieced together Aunt Jennifer's story.

She'd been engaged to her high school sweetheart, a guy named Dan. There were nice pictures in the local paper announcing their engagement. There was a frilly and fancy save-the-date card for their wedding. And then there was a brief obituary announcing his death.

After that, I guess, Aunt Jennifer was called to action. She was called to protest against war and violence and U.S. occupations of other countries. From the looks of it, she spent half a decade traveling the world and working for peace organizations.

And then, there were no more papers.

It's like she took off the blue face paint and hung up her nun outfit or maybe burned it, 'cause I sure didn't see it amidst her clothes. It seemed as if she took all the paint off her face and spread it all around her new blue house in her little subdivision in the little suburb of Urbandale, Iowa.

Suddenly, I felt tears rolling down my cheeks again. I'd cried more in the past month than the previous thirteen years of my life. Real tears. Big, huge crocodile tears like the kind Aunt Jennifer painted on her face in memory of her fiancé. I cried for my aunt. I cried for her life. I cried because she quit protesting. I cried because I had killed her.

I lay back on the blue carpet and stared at the ceiling and let the tears go until they were sliding down the sides of my face and into my ear. The tears filled my ear canal until I couldn't hear anymore. They pooled up in my ear canal so I didn't hear Cecilia come through the back door.

Also, I had my eyes closed, so I didn't see it coming when she started hitting me.

CHAPTER 15

"What are you doing!?" I screamed.

Cecilia had come up from behind and started slapping at my head and then began to punch my shoulders and my chest with her closed fists.

"Stop it! Cut it out!"

It took me awhile to get up, but I eventually got to my knees as she continued pounding. I was sitting there like some sort of dog on my hands and knees with her still pounding away at me, but I exploded into a standing position and then tackled her. It took her by surprise this time. And even though I knew she had martial arts in her or something, I was able to get the best of Cecilia and pin her to the ground.

"What the hell are you doing?" I asked.

She just glared at me and it was like I was staring into her father's eyes instead of hers. They were black, soulless pits and they just looked right through me. I couldn't believe how dead her eyes looked. I had all of my weight on top of Cecilia. I pinned her down tight. She only tried to wriggle free once or twice. She didn't say anything either. Just stared at me.

"Why did you hit me? What's wrong with you? Are you pissed about something?"

But she didn't answer. She just stared at me for awhile and then she shook her head a little like she was done with the whole thing. Then she turned her head to the side and closed her eyes and I could feel her body go limp under me.

I sat there on top of her for a very long time. I'll be honest and admit that I was a little scared to get up. I was afraid that if I moved, she might tense up and spring back to life and start whaling on me again. So I sat there with my butt pinning down her skinny legs and my hands gripping her upper arms. Finally, I started to loosen my hold a little and she stayed limp and unmoving. Her breathing had slowed way down almost like she was sleeping or something.

I lifted my hands completely off her and sat up and quit leaning forward. I still sat on her legs, but I lifted my weight off of her a little bit too.

"Cecilia?" I said softly. "Are you all right?"

She still didn't answer, but she also wasn't trying to attack me, so I slowly lifted my left leg and swung it around so that I was completely off her. Then I sat down cross-legged beside Cecilia and watched her breathing slow even more.

Maybe it was some sort of an attack. Maybe she had a brain disease, like epilepsy. This was some a seizure or something.

"Cecilia?"

She sighed and then turned her head just a little bit. The tiniest of little bits actually.

And then, even though it made no sense at all, it suddenly struck me that this had something to do with her mother. It was like I just knew. This had something to do with her mother dying of cancer and all. I don't know how the thought snuck into my head, but sometimes a thought will just creep in like that and it's so obvious and your brain just knows that's the deal. Your brain is totally sure that something is true. If I believed in God, like my dad did, or like I even think Cecilia did, I'd say that this kind of thought was the kind of thing God planted in my brain. It was like a thought that had nothing to do with anything. I couldn't have come up with a thought like this on my own.

I reached my hand out to touch Cecilia's hair and the moment my fingers made contact, her chest moved a little. Her chest was like an ocean or something and it started to ripple a little as if a wave was coming in. And then it started to ripple more like some bigger waves were on the way. And then, it lifted as if a tsunami was approaching and the biggest wave of all slammed into Cecilia's head and her eyes flew open and she stared at me, only this time her eyes were back and her father's eyes were gone. And the tsunami wave came pouring out of her eyes and she opened her mouth and it came pouring out of her mouth too and she was full-on crying.

Wailing, for that matter.

I let my fingers slowly stroke her hair and it felt so soft. Her hair was the softest thing I'd ever touched and for some reason, I was surprised that it felt so soft and I was surprised that I'd never known that about her. I'd never touched Cecilia's hair before and never knew that her hair was softer than silk. It felt like dipping my hand in a warm tub of water, and opening my fingers wide and stirring.

I uncrossed my legs and lay down beside her and continued to stroke Cecilia's hair while she stared at me and cried and after awhile, her eyes drooped and she pretty much just fell asleep and I pretty much fell asleep, too. When we woke up it was like two in the morning.

"Thank you," she said.

"That's okay. Why were you so upset?"

"I guess I was afraid that you were going to leave me like my mother did."

I was totally shocked by that answer, and honestly I didn't know what I should say. I caught myself frowning at her like I was annoyed with what she said, but I was mostly surprised.

"Your father is probably pretty worried about you right now," I told her.

"He thinks I went to bed early."

"Doesn't he ever check up on you in the middle of the night? Make sure you didn't run off to cause problems?"

Cecilia's expression melted from curiosity to amusement and then quickly into waves of laughter. I was surprised when she started laughing, but I got swept up in the wave too and soon we were both just cracking up on the floor. Rolling around. Caught up in the ridiculousness of the idea that Cecilia would ever get up to some sort of mischief.

Of course, this was all before she did.

CHAPTER 16

For two whole days, we pretty much hid out in my aunt's house. Cecilia went home super early in the morning so her father would find her there when he woke up. But she skipped school and hung out with me and she told him she was having dinner with me and she'd come over and we'd raid my aunt's food.

"Are you going to call and find out how your aunt is doing?" Cecilia asked me several times over those days.

"I'd rather not."

"She's probably still alive, you know. Otherwise they would have come here to her house. Looked through her things. Found a dress for the funeral and stuff like that."

"I suppose."

"You should let me call and ask."

I didn't answer her when she made this offer. I really didn't want her to call and I really didn't want to deal with the truth when she found out. Plus, I know the minute she called my parents they'd realize I was probably hanging out with her and they'd track us down. Either that or Cecilia wouldn't be able to meet me anymore because they'd be following her every move.

"I don't have to call your parents. I could just call the hospital and say I'm a relative."

I considered it, but it seemed unlikely that they'd release any information to her. I shook my head.

"C'mon, just let me try."

She picked up her phone and scrolled through the contacts until she found the hospital.

"Why do you have the hospital number on your phone?"

"I called and checked in on her the day after she was

admitted."

I nodded. Of course she did.

"Hi, I just want to check on the status of my aunt, Jennifer Driscoll. Sure. I'll hold." Cecilia smiled at me while we waited. "Yes. Yes. Yes. Okay. No, I didn't know that. Okay. Thanks."

She hung up her phone and looked over to me. I couldn't tell if her expression was happy, sad, or none of the above.

"She's doing all right. I guess she had some sort of brain aneurysm so she went into surgery yesterday."

I nodded and didn't know if I was happy, sad or none of the above.

"What else did they say?"

"The woman said that visiting hours were until seven p.m. if I wanted to stop by and visit her."

"Oh."

We sat there in silence for a long time. I knew what she wanted me to do. But I wasn't ready.

"Hey, wanna look through some of her old newspaper clippings?"

I shrugged and followed Cecilia's lead.

She opened one of the magazines on top and turned to the page that had been bookmarked using an old-fashioned cassette tape in a plastic box.

"Listen to this ... the Blue Nun has been known to climb over barbed wire and stand in front of moving tanks. At the G8 summit in Munich, she ignored direct orders from a battalion of soldiers and continued her march to the gates of the compound where the summit was being held. She then gripped the steel bars of the compound fence and sang a hymn. You could hear a pin drop, when, by the time she reached the first chorus, her haunting voice silencing the angry protesters and young Marines alike. By the time she reached the second chorus, all of the protesters and half the Marines had joined in: 'Amazing Grace, how sweet the sound, that saved a wretch like me. I once was lost but now am found, was blind, but now I see.'"

Cecilia opened the case and removed the tape, which was marked with the words Munich 1992.

"Does your aunt have a tape player somewhere?"

"Sure. There's a boom box down in the kitchen with one."

We headed downstairs, clicked the tape into place in the machine, and hit play.

We stood with slack jaws and listened, much as the crowd did when my aunt finished singing. It was ethereal. It was heavenly. It was divine and sublime and celestial. The crowd was silent when she finished singing. They remained silent for what seemed like minutes and you could hear people sobbing. Then, one lone person began clapping and others joined in and the crowd went into a frenzy of applause and congratulations. The applause seemed to last longer than the song.

"That's incredible. Your aunt is like a folk hero."

"Folk singer."

"Both."

"I suppose."

"Do you ever want to accomplish something huge like that?" Cecilia asked me.

"Not really." I paused because I knew that answer was not totally true and also because Ian had recently hit me with a similar question. "I mean. What could I accomplish?"

"I don't know. Maybe you could do like her. You're very talented at doing sneaky things ... maybe you could...."

"What is that supposed to mean ... 'sneaky things?' What in the hell are you trying to say?"

She smiled in a way that told me she hadn't intended anything mean or bad.

"I actually respect your sneakiness. I was simply thinking you'd be good at some sort of domestic terrorism or something similar that could make a big statement."

"You're full of it. What in the hell are you talking about?"

I was totally confused about the whole conversation. I swear it seemed as if she was serious. This didn't seem like a joke, but at the same time it was certainly strange coming out of the mouth of Miss Goody Two-Shoes.

"I'm just saying. My dad and I were talking last week about how ... you know ... how all these haters are out there in the world and it's so sad. People like my mother and your aunt who truly cared about other human beings and put in all this effort to make the world a better place and make people quit hurting each other and all their work leads to nothing."

"Your mom? Was she a protester too?"

"Sort of. She used to write letters to people. Used to do all kinds of phone calls to Congress and things like that. Especially after she got sick."

"What about?"

"Oh. Everything, you know. Stuff about getting troops out of the Middle East and expanding library hours. You name it."

"She sounds like she was a good person," I said and I meant it. I'm not prone to saying a bunch of sappy crap, but I could tell that Cecilia truly loved her mother and I wanted to point it out to her. Point out that her mother sounded very nice.

Instead of thanking me, though, or breaking down crying about her mother, Cecilia acted almost like I hadn't said a word. She simply stared ahead at the pictures and articles in my aunt's drawer. Then she sprung it on me:

"Olivia, I was thinking that seriously we should do something. Do something radical."

"Like what?"

She paused and then got a very stern look on her face. "You know the City Hall steps where all of those idiots like your dad are protesting?"

"Sure."

"I think we should bomb the place. Go in there with backpacks filled with explosives and blow it up. Make a big statement."

Now, I never knew Cecilia to make many jokes, and she said it with a totally straight face and I was ... well ... I was taken aback. I didn't know how to respond to something like that. Obviously, she was joking around. She was, wasn't she?

She got a big grin and punched me in the shoulder. "Obviously I'm just joking around, you know. The radical thing I was actually thinking about is starting a band."

I laughed because I knew that I was supposed to.

I laughed because if I didn't laugh, things would have become very awkward between us and Cecilia was truly the first best friend I'd ever had. She was my only friend.

"Yeah. Let's start a band." I said.

She added: "We'll blast those fuckers off the City Hall steps with big amplifiers."

CHAPTER 17

Of course, before we could get on with our lives and start a band, I had to deal with my aunt. It was a problem that wasn't going away.

Cecilia convinced me to go out there and visit the hospital, though I was very afraid of what I'd find.

As it turned out, my aunt was alive and talking and she was worried sick about me.

"Olivia!" Aunt Jennifer said.

Mom and Dad just kinda looked at the two of us and didn't seem too excited to see me.

"Where have you been? We've been worried sick. You haven't been staying at Cecilia's the whole time, have you?"

She gave Cecilia a sideways glance and a slight frown, but I think she knew even as she asked it, that Cecilia wouldn't have lied to them all when asked about it.

I shook my head. "I've been staying at your house, Aunt Jennifer."

In my peripheral vision, I could see Mom and Dad shaking their heads back and forth.

"We were worried sick, you know," Aunt Jennifer said, though it didn't really look like Mom and Dad gave a rat's ass.

Dad looked like he was simply worn out, or hungover. His eyes were puffy and bloodshot and he squinted at me as though he could barely make out that I existed. That's how it often was with him, though. He seemed to either be loud and boisterous and tossing me around, or else he was spacing out like I didn't even exist.

My aunt gave me a big hug and as she did it, the IV tubes

stretched and it made the IV stand squeak and wheeled along the floor a little bit. I backed up and held her at arm's length and asked her the question I'd been scared to ask for weeks. "Are you going to die?"

She laughed and told me no.

For their part, Mom and Dad hung out against the wall and didn't say anything. I saw Dad's eyes closing and he was drifting and I totally realized that he was hungover. My first instinct had been right. For some reason, this annoyed the crap out of me. I turned to Cecilia and it seemed obvious that she noticed the same thing about him. I decided at that moment that I wanted the hell out of there.

"Well, I'm glad you're not dead, Aunt Jennifer. I just wanted to stop by and make sure everything is OK. I'm going back home, now."

As Cecilia and I turned to leave, Mom reached her hand out and put it on my shoulder. When she spoke, she spoke very softly, but there was something strong about it. I'd never heard her speak with so much seriousness.

"Olivia, we want you to come back and stay at the apartment with us for awhile."

"But what about Aunt Jennifer's?"

"Maybe after your aunt is feeling better and returns home, you can stay with her some, but you're not old enough to be taking care of yourself."

I looked her in the eyes, and despite the seriousness in her voice and everything else, I couldn't help but laugh. I wasn't old enough to take care of myself? I'd been taking care of myself since I was a little kid. For that matter, I'd been taking care of them since I was a little kid.

"Sorry. I'm going back to Aunt Jennifer's."

I walked out the door.

Cecilia and I walked without talking and jumped on a bus. I remembered what she said about doing something with my life. I also remembered what Ian said about making a difference in the world.

"I have a better idea than going to my aunt's house."

Cecilia shrugged and agreed to come along. We got off the

bus at Merle Hay Mall and I dragged her down to the food court. Sure enough, Ian was there playing Joust as if I'd never left him. Cecilia and I stood behind him for some time and then I cleared my throat loudly, even though I knew he could see my face like a mirror in his game.

I saw the reflection of his smile.

"Ian, I want to introduce you to my friend here."

He took his hand off the game long enough to toss a wave over his shoulder, but he was too involved to actually pause the game. Still, he was smiling a broad smile and that sent a few shivers up and down my spine.

We stood there for a long time waiting for the game to finish. Eventually, I walked up to the clerk and bought a root beer for me and Cecilia to share. I was kind of annoyed that Ian just sat there playing the stupid game, but when he finally died, I cut him some slack because I saw why he was so engrossed.

"Hell yeah!"

"Did you play well?" Cecilia asked him.

"Beat my top score."

"Which is something like twice as much as anyone else's top score," I added, just to brag a bit on Ian.

"Anyway, sorry to blow you off like that," he said while extending his hand to Cecilia. She shook it and he gave her some sort of a little winky, squint-eyed smile. I was glad that Ian was so charming and glad that he seemed to work his magic on my friend.

"Ian, this is my friend."

As he shook her hand, he asked her the question that I knew would come up, but I didn't really want to deal with. "What's your name?"

"My name's Cecilia," she answered.

Ian screwed up his face into a sort of topographical map with lines and peaks and valleys all over it.

"You're both named Cecilia?"

Then it was Cecilia's turn, though her screwed-up face seemed to smile more and therefore more closely resembled a laughing hyena than a topographical map.

"Not exactly," I began. "My name is actually Olivia. I was just pulling your leg when I said it was Cecilia."

He scrunched his face even more. "I guess both names end in i-a."

Cecilia started laughing. "Why did you say you were me?"

"I guess I figured that way if Ian turns out to be some sort of crazy stalker, he'll go after you instead of me."

"Okay, then, Olivia. To what do I owe the pleasure of your visit here today?" he asked.

"Well, this is the deal, Ian: you were telling me how you were some sort of musical prodigy, and Cecilia and I need some help with starting a band."

"We do?" Cecilia asked.

I nodded.

"What kind of band?"

I answered "hip-hop" at the same instant that Cecilia answered "emo."

"Jinx," I said.

"You can't say jinx unless we say the same thing at the same time. Not two different things at the same time."

"So what do I say if it's not jinx?"

"Klinx," Ian answered, and for some reason, his stupid joke, which was barely even a joke, totally cracked us up. To the point that I ended up snorting root beer out my nose which burned like you wouldn't believe. This caused Cecilia to practically spit a huge spray of root beer from her mouth, though she mostly held it in and only a minor eruption happened.

"Gimme some of that root beer," Ian demanded. "I need to see if I can send root beer spitting out of any of my body orifices."

This set the round of laughter into motion again, especially as he turned and squatted toward us with his butt sticking out like he was going to shoot a fart our way. The way he did it seemed a little gay, but I was pretty sure Ian was a straight kid.

I hoped Ian was a straight kid. He was funny like a gay kid, though.

We laughed so hard and spit so much that the owner of the little deli eventually asked the three of us to leave. At least he did it in a nice way with a smile and a shake of his head that said: Oh, you crazy kids. I remember when I was young. Ha, ha, ha.

We bounded from the mall with nothing better to do than

hop from store to store and lean over the railing of the mezzanine and stare at the people in the food court below. As we stared down, Cecilia got a devilish look in her eye and pointed out the cleavage of a buxom middle-aged woman.

"Do either of you have any gum?"

"Gum?" I asked.

"Um...." I dug around in my purse until I found a stick and handed it to her.

Cecilia unwrapped it, chewed it up, and then dangled the pink blob from the end of her finger as if she were about to drop it between the woman's breasts.

"You wouldn't," Ian said with wide eyes.

"Would you?" I asked.

And with another devilish grin, Cecilia let loose and the pink blob dropped like a heavy weight, veered slightly to the left, bounced against some fat guy's bald head, and ricocheted off the woman's left boob.

Surprisingly, neither the bald guy nor the woman glanced up in the air toward us, but instead looked around as if there was somebody across the room who'd shot the gum at them from some sort of a gum rifle. But then, Ian had to ruin everything and let out a big laugh. This caused the lady and the guy to look up at the mezzanine and stare directly at us.

Cecilia was the first to duck down out of the way, followed by me and then I had to pull on Ian to get him to come along. We ran down past the Mrs. Fields store and that place that sells the giant kettles of popcorn that nobody ever buys except at Christmas time. As we rounded the corner by the Orange Julius, we came face to face with the big-boobed woman and her bald husband, who were now accompanied by a mall cop with a cheesy little mustache.

"Hey, you kids!" he yelled. He sounded like some goofball from an old Disney movie. And like the three crazy kids from the same movie, Cecilia and Ian and I turned and ran with our feet skittering across the slick floor.

I could hear the security guy calling for backup on his walkie-talkie, but I was pretty certain that even a whole passel of mall cops wouldn't keep up with the likes of us. By the time we reached the parking lot, all the walkie-talkie talk was far in the distance. Still, we ran all the way to the Casey's General Store anyway.

"Let's get some ice cream." Ian suggested and Cecilia and I thought that sounded like a fine idea.

I got a Choco-Taco, Ian bought a Push-up and Cecilia, of course, chose a Frozen Juice bar made with 100 percent juice and no high-fructose corn syrup.

"You're not on some kind of a diet, are you?" Ian asked her.

"No, but I try to avoid foods that are bad for me."

We sat on the same curb stop that Cecilia and I had when the idiot in the truck practically killed us. We licked our frozen treats and didn't talk for a long time. Didn't talk even as the sun dipped down behind the houses and the trees.

CHAPTER 18

Cecilia and I walked Ian home.

Ian, who, despite being older, had a curfew and had to be in his house just after dark. We said goodbye at his driveway and Ian was polite, the perfect gentleman, to both of us.

"Nice to meet you, Cecilia," he said as he shook her hand.

"And, as always, nice to see you again, Cecilia the second, or should I say, Olivia," he said as he lifted the back of my hand to his lips and gave it a little kiss while lifting his eyes and looking up at me at the same time. Now, I'm no sort of girly-girl, but Ian's little move made my cheeks blush, flush, and otherwise rush with red.

As we walked away from his house, I could feel Cecilia's eyes burning a hole in me from the side. She was smart enough, though, to wait until we were out of Ian's earshot.

"I think he's in love with you," she said with only a bit of a smile.

You'd have thought she would say it with a little more enthusiasm, but I guess Cecilia was a pretty even-keeled girl even when it came to things like this.

"You think so?" I asked while attempting to hide my obvious excitement at the prospect.

Of course, I'd thought and hoped that for some time now, but there was something very satisfying about having someone outside of my own brain bring this up.

"Are you just playing dumb, Olivia?"

"No, I mean I kind of thought that he may think of me in that way, but you never know and well ... it's just a surprise to hear someone else say that they think something like that."

"What else would I think? First, he is like some typical guy at the mall—all aloof and acting like he couldn't care at all about you. Then at the end, he's kissing your hand and making you blush. That's how boys do it, you know That's part of the whole mating ritual—act like they don't give a crap and then go in for the kill. The mating dance. Swing your partner out far away and then pull her in close and squeeze her until she's ready to pop."

"Mating? We're not mating. We're just flirting around a little bit."

"Well, whatever … it's really a mating ritual, whether you like to think of it that way or not."

Why in the world did Cecilia have to turn something nice and fun into so much stuff to have to think about? She could suck the fun right out of a room sometimes. We walked on for awhile and I got to feeling a little bit peeved about her and her way of being so much better than everyone else. Again, there she was trying to tell me that it wasn't okay just to be happy and have fun. I had to dissect it all and analyze it and turn it into something more than it needed to be. Sometimes Cecilia could be a total pain in the butt.

"Do you want to talk about it?" She asked.

I guess it was obvious that I was huffing and puffing.

"Not really."

We walked another block or so.

"You know it's not good to keep it all bottled up inside. It's not good for your health. That's how people end up with all kinds of physical problems."

I couldn't help myself. "You mean like cancer?"

"Exactly," she said as if not even noticing my harsh dig.

We walked another block.

"I'm sorry." I told her.

"That's okay. It's true … what you said about cancer. Cancer comes from internalized anger, you know."

"Oh."

"My mother should have let it out more often. Let people know what she was feeling, but instead she bottled it up inside and it ate away at her until she died from it."

"Oh."

"I'm afraid I have some of the same problem. You know.

91

Inside of me."

"Cancer?"

"No. Not so much cancer. I just think I probably have a lot of anger inside me."

"About your mother?"

"Yeah. And probably some other things. Some bigger things like the state of the world."

"Do you think you may get cancer from it?"

"I don't know. I don't want to."

"What are you going to do to stop it?"

"I think I need to channel it into something that will help the world."

"Like our band? It may not help the whole world, but it may help a few kids like us."

She stopped walking and turned to me like she had something important to say. She stated into my eyes. She looked like she may have been on the verge of tears. But then she turned again and started walking.

"Yeah. Like our band," she said.

And then the whole mood of the evening changed. The sun was all the way down behind the trees and we were getting close to my aunt's house. It was as if Cecilia just flipped some switch inside of her brain. Some switch that made her go from morose and contemplative to the wacky, excited girl who'd just thrown the chewed-up gum at some fat woman's boob.

"What should we call the band? I've always liked the name Shanghai Buddhist Youth, or maybe Velvet Belly. We could do like a performance up there on the stage. Not just sing and play instruments, but really put on a show. I went to an all-ages show in West Des Moines once where this woman was up on stage singing in this really shrill, haunting voice and she looked like she was really big and beefy, fat even, and as she sang each song, she pulled out a huge kitchen knife and started to cut off the dress she was wearing, only underneath that was another dress. And with each song, she cut off the next dress down, until you thought maybe she was going to go all the way down to her underwear. You didn't really know. And she just kept cutting off dresses and playing and...."

Cecilia said all of this in one long breath and I thought maybe she did have a way that she was able to let some of her anger seep out. It seemed like that was exactly what she was up to right now. Probably what she was up to when she hit the boob with the gum.

"Did she do it?" I asked.

"Do what? Cut herself?" Cecilia replied.

"No. Why cut herself? Why would I think she'd cut herself? I wanted to know, did she cut off all of her clothes?"

"Oh, I forgot to tell you that before she cut off each dress, she would drag the knife across her skin, her neck and arms and stuff. She sort of acted like she was going to slit her own throat or something. Or cut her wrists. But she didn't."

"Did she cut off all of her clothes, though?"

"I don't remember."

I was flabbergasted. "What do you mean you don't remember? You can't remember whether or not some lady cut off all of her clothes in front of an audience. How can you not remember that?"

Cecilia shrugged.

There was another long pause. While my mind imagined the scene, we stopped walking and Cecilia turned to look at me.

"Do you think Ian is going to be your boyfriend?"

"I suppose maybe. Who knows how these mating rituals work." I grinned and Cecilia grinned too.

I turned as if I was going to keep walking, but Cecilia kept facing me, so I turned back toward her.

"You know, we're going to need all sorts of equipment to get a band going. Besides instruments, we'll need amps and recording equipment and a bunch of stuff like that and it isn't cheap."

"I don't think we have to worry about that yet. We don't even know how to play one song."

"I'm just saying. With Ian helping us, we'll be good in no time and we'll need equipment and that's where you're going to come in handy."

"What do you mean, I'll come in handy?"

"I mean your talents will come in handy."

I knew what she was getting at, but I could barely believe it.

"You mean you actually want me to steal things?"

"Sometimes ... I think ... it's okay to do something morally questionable if it serves a larger purpose."

"You're saying the ends justify the means?" I asked.

"Sort of. I just mean that the ends justify the means when it's for a big political cause like this. The ends justify the means when there are lives at stake."

"Political cause? Lives at stake? I thought we were just starting a band?"

This time, it was Cecilia's turn to begin walking. When she did it, of course, I just followed.

"What instrument are you going to play?" She asked me.

"I hadn't thought too much about it. I figured I'd let Ian decide."

"Can you sing?" she asked.

"Not really. I think I could probably sing backup. But I wouldn't want to sing the front part. Or lead, or whatever it's called."

"That's all right. I'll be lead singer and dress-cutter." Cecilia said with a smile.

"I dare you to be bra and underwear cutter," I said with an elbow jab.

"You think I'd be afraid of that? Hell, I'll be wrist-cutter too. I'm not afraid of anything." She answered.

I knew in that moment that Cecilia truly wasn't afraid of anything. I used to think that I wasn't afraid of anything, but I'd learned a lot about fear over the past few months and now realized that everything I thought about me and Cecilia was now turned upside down on its head.

CHAPTER 19

I'd never been nervous about stealing anything before, and I think it may have been because I'd always done it alone. Except maybe, the first time when I was like in first grade and me and a friend grabbed some candy at a little drugstore. My friend freaked out that time. It was too long ago to remember her name. I just remember talking her into doing it and then when we left the drugstore she seemed all mad at me.

"What's the problem?"

"You made me do it. I'm telling my mom that you made me steal this."

"I didn't make you do anything. Did I put your hand on that Snickers bar and force it into your pocket?" I'd heard Dad say similar things a hundred times before.

She yelled like a little baby, threw the candy bar down on the ground, and ran all the way home to her mommy.

As Cecilia and I pushed through the basement window of the First Methodist Church on Merle Hay and 63rd, I felt more like my little friend than I did like myself. And then, I got to thinking back to some things Aunt Jennifer had said to me and I started to put two and two together.

"Cecilia! This isn't just any church. I think this is the church my aunt goes to on Sundays."

"So. What does that matter?"

"Maybe it doesn't, but I'm not so sure that stealing from any church is such a good idea. And on a Sunday, no less."

"What do you mean? You used to steal from all kinds of people. You stole my bike and my family is poor. The good thing about stealing from a church is that they're rich. They have hundreds of people, probably, who can chip in and buy them new stuff. Besides, Sunday night is the best time to do it since nobody will notice anything is missing for a whole week."

"Still, aren't you worried that ... I don't know. Maybe God will strike us dead or something."

Cecilia just laughed.

She laughed as she jumped through the window and landed beside me on the cold, painted concrete floor.

"Do you really believe in God?" She asked.

"I don't know, but it might be good to at least entertain the idea when you're in the middle of breaking into a church. You know, do a little risk assessment."

She laughed at me again. "Where did you hear about risk assessment?"

I was totally put out by her question. "I'm not stupid, Cecilia. You know I was in TAG at my old school and you know that I get in the 95th percentile whenever I take tests. I'm not sure why you always treat me like I'm a moron."

She pushed out her lower lip in some kind of a pout. "I'm sorry. I didn't mean to hurt your feelings."

"You didn't hurt my feelings. I'm just saying, 95th percentile."

"I just sometimes forget that 95th percentile is still really smart since I scored in the 98th."

I just laughed because I saw how ridiculous this conversation was. "Well, don't forget, Cecilia, that there is someone out there in the 99th percentile and they could make you their bitch."

She cracked up at that too, until we heard a creaking floorboard above us in the church and stopped dead in our tracks. I turned to skitter up the wall and leave through the same window that we'd just entered, but Cecilia grabbed my ankle as I started to pull myself up.

"Shhhh...." she said, and we both turned our heads and aimed our ears at the ceiling like a couple of church rats. Which, I suppose we were.

The creaking sound moved, one step at a time, above our heads and headed in the direction of the stairs that would lead whoever it was down to us. The person stopped at the stairs and didn't move for a long time. Cecilia and I froze in place too.

And then, as if she had some sort of ESP, Cecilia held up four fingers and mouthed a countdown as she lowered them one at a time. "Four ... three ... two..." and at one, I heard the clicking sound of a lock and then the floorboards began creaking in the opposite direction as the person decided to leave the basement alone.

Now, more than ever, I was ready to head out that window, but this time Cecilia grabbed my arm and whispered in my ear: "C'mon. We don't have much time now. His show is starting."

At that moment, I heard the sound of canned television laughter from upstairs and I realized that Cecilia didn't have any sort of ESP. She had been here before to stake the place out. Probably last Sunday.

"Who is he?"

"It's Mr. Crenshaw."

"That old perv that paid me to come in his house and show me his thing?"

"No," she answered. "Mr. Crenshaw, the guy you made up a story about being an old perv who paid you to come in his house and show you his thing."

Sometimes I forgot which stuff I tell people is a lie and which stuff is truth.

"Mr. Crenshaw gets paid to clean up and then he spends the night at the church on Sunday nights to make sure nobody messes with the collection before he can get it to the bank first thing Monday morning."

"Won't he notice all of the musical equipment and stuff missing?"

"No, the first thing he cleans is the basement. He already finished down here. And then when he's done cleaning the upstairs, he walks over to the door and latches it and locks himself in for the night with the collection plate and watches some TV shows."

I was incredulous. Had Cecilia actually done all this staking out and spying and casing the joint?

"I don't have a good feeling about this, Cecilia."

"Why not? I made sure we wouldn't have any surprises."

I thought about why this all felt so wrong. "I think that's my problem. I don't know how to do this stuff that way."

"What do you mean?"

"I always swiped things because I wanted them right then. It always felt more like some sort of primal urge. I would see something that I wanted and then I'd grab it. There's something about all this planning and scheming that feels … well … it feels wrong. And a church? And some old guy upstairs hiding with a collection plate? I just feel a little strange about this whole thing."

"Don't tell me you're getting cold feet?"

"I don't know. I'm simply saying that this feels wrong."

Cecilia looked at me as if there was something wrong with me. She stared with an odd expression like she was trying to figure out what to do next.

"I hear what you're saying, Olivia. I totally do." She paused and scrunched up her face in more thought. "I think I understand what this is really all about. This is your intuition speaking to you. And I should probably listen to it."

"You should?"

"Well … I'm saying that I probably should, but I may not in this case. Listen: you've stolen things a lot more often than I have and you're more attuned to the way something like this is supposed to feel. I can use all the logic in the world, but your intuition is obviously better than mine on this stuff."

"You say you should listen to me, but you're not going to?"

"I should listen to you, and I don't want you to get in trouble for my stupidity, but it's very important that we get this stuff tonight. We need to start practicing and if we don't get this thing together soon, it could be too late."

"Too late for what?"

She bit her lip, and the minute she did, I knew that I wasn't going to get an answer.

"I'm just saying that I need to do this tonight, but I think you should trust your intuition," She waved toward the open window. "Go on home and I'll get the stuff."

I looked at the window, but the only pull I felt was toward Cecilia. "I'll help, but let's make this fast."

She smiled and slid across the basement floor as gracefully as a bird gliding over the water. We gathered up microphones and microphone stands and a couple of heavy amplifiers. We quietly carried them toward the window and left them on the floor below it. We then headed back and grabbed a keyboard and a couple of guitar cases—one with a bass and the other with a regular guitar. We set them in the same place. On our last trip, Cecilia looked in a couple of suitcases and we discovered all sorts of cables and pedals and wires and things that neither of us knew anything about. We grabbed them since Cecilia was sure we would need that stuff too.

We looked at the equipment that was left and decided most of it wasn't worth taking. We didn't need a drum kit since Ian already had one. There were also couple of huge amps that were simply too big to fit through the window.

Then Cecilia and I noticed the green case at the same time. It had been leaned up against the bass drum and looked too short to be a guitar. We headed over there and Cecilia slowly opened the case to reveal a dulcimer. Neither of us knew much about dulcimers except that they were the preferred instrument of hippy-dippy fifth-grade music teachers. For whatever reason, Cecilia just had to have it.

"Why in the hell would you want that thing?"

"Are you serious? It's a dulcimer."

She sealed it up and grabbed the ugly green case and heaved it through the window before helping me escape the basement.

As she boosted me up through the window, I caught my arm on a sharp corner of aluminum window frame. It scraped the length of skin from my wrist to my elbow and I looked down to see a gaping wound of pink flesh that had opened up to the world.

I stared at my skin and expected to see blood. Instead, my arm looked like it belonged to some dead body on a slab in one of those crime scene cop shows. The skin separated and no blood came out. I simply saw a wide pink slit and began to feel like I was going to barf.

Then my heart must have decided to beat because the pink slit filled with blood and then I did barf. I threw up all over the lawn outside the window. I dry-heaved a couple more times and then wiped the puke from my lips and flung it with the back of my hand.

"Are you all right?"

"Yeah, just start passing the stuff up here. We gotta go."

As she began to heave the first amp, I looked again at the gaping wound. I was bleeding, but it wasn't gushing out or anything. The blood simply dripped down my hand and slowly drip-dropped off my fingers. I took the equipment and carefully stacked it into the two HyVee shopping carts we'd left next to the building.

The wound looked bad, but I wasn't bleeding to death. I'd probably need stitches, though.

After the last thing was loaded into the cart, I reached down to grab Cecilia's hand and help her up through the window, but she paused and looked back over her shoulder.

"C'mon," I said. "We gotta go!"

"I'm sorry, Olivia, but there's one more thing I gotta do here."

"What do you mean? We have to get out of here!"

"I'm sorry. I didn't tell you about this part, because I thought you might not go for it. But I need to do one more thing. Please just grab one of the shopping carts and follow the path I told you to get to my house. My father won't be home for another half hour, but you have to hurry. I'll get the other cart and be a few minutes behind you."

"But Cecilia...." She cut me off by closing the window from the inside. She latched it, obviously wanting to make sure I didn't follow her.

I peered through the window and tried to see past the darkness to see what she was up to. For some reason, a crazy thought popped into my head: She was going to torch the place to hide the evidence. I don't know why I thought it. Something about that image of the monk on fire in Cecilia's locker came into my head.

But then, I saw glimpses of her as she moved toward the stairs and I realized where she was headed.

She was going after the collection plate.

I grabbed the shopping cart and ran. If I would've had a candy bar instead of a shopping cart, I would have thrown it on the ground and run all the way home to my mommy.

CHAPTER 20

"I had to do it, you know." Cecilia told me when she arrived at her house. "There will be expenses. We'll need things beside equipment."

The collection plate was actually a collection bag and when Cecilia dumped it out on top of the amplifier in her father's garage, I was impressed with the haul. A few coins bounced off the amp and skittered this way and that across the garage floor— probably some little kids had tossed them in there. But most of the money was bills. And they weren't small bills either. There were fives and tens and a few fifties, but mostly twenties and there were more than I could count. This was some sort of a rich church and these people weren't afraid of getting poor.

The pile of loot sat loosely atop the amp, with a few bills sliding off the top of the pile and drifting to the ground like feathers. Expensive feathers.

"How much is there?" I asked.

"I don't know yet. This is the first I've looked at it. Could be a grand or more."

We started piling the bills together. Cecilia turned hers this way and that because she wanted them all to face a certain direction. I was content to simply pile them one atop the other.

When we were done with the piling and had picked up the loose change, we had a total of $1,243.14.

"Not a bad haul. When you start adding up the price of the amps and guitars and equipment, I think we have close to ten grand here." She spoke with a broad smile.

I didn't know what to say. I just stared at all the money.

"Here." She extended her hand and tried to give me all the

money.

"Why are you giving it to me?"

"I've got all the equipment here in my father's garage. It's only fair that you should hold some of the loot."

"No thanks."

"C'mon, Olivia. You took as big a chance as me. You can even treat yourself to something. Maybe a hundred bucks or so. We'll need most of it for other things, but we can spare some of it for something fun."

My stomach was in knots even more than when we first crawled through the church window. "No thanks," was all I could say.

"Well ... will you be here tomorrow for practice?"

"Here?"

"Sure. I told my father that we were going to practice over here."

"How will you explain all this new musical stuff?"

"I told him that Ian was going to bring his equipment over. I said that Ian had the equipment, but didn't have a place that he could practice."

"I'm not sure we're ready to bring Ian into all this." I was feeling nervous about Ian and all the theft stuff, but Cecilia seemed to read my mind.

"Don't worry. I told Ian that I borrowed the equipment from a friend of my father's."

"I don't know, Cecilia. I feel a bit lightheaded trying to keep track of all of this. It's too many lies. We're so going to get busted."

Suddenly, Cecilia looked down at the floor and her gaze slowly lifted from my feet up the length of my legs to my hand. A look of surprise overtook her face.

"Oh my god, Olivia. You're bleeding!"

My gaze followed hers to the floor and I saw a circle of blood the size of a small saucer. I immediately began to feel nauseous again. I felt my face turning green.

"What did you do to yourself? Are you OK?"

"Oh, it's nothing. Just a little cut." As I said it, I lifted the sleeve of my torn shirt and exposed the wound, which was now looking a little puffy and swollen and … well … not so good. The room began to turn and, before I knew it, I was headed for the floor, though Cecilia braced against me with her shoulder and helped me over to the amp to sit down.

"You need stitches at the very least," she said. "We need to get you to the doctor."

"We can't … I mean … the police may already know about the break-in and they may have found the window where I cut myself. They may already be canvassing the neighborhood for someone with a cut just like this."

"Get real, Olivia. This isn't a cop movie and that's not a gunshot wound. We'll tell them that you slipped on something. C'mon."

"How?"

"What do you mean, how?"

"I mean, how are we going to get there?"

She looked over to the corner of the garage. Her dad's motorcycle. For a minute, when I realized what was about to happen, I began to feel like my old self. Cecilia was going to take me on the motorcycle. A tingle moved up my spine.

The last time I'd ridden a motorcycle was something like five years ago when Dad went through a biker phase while we were living out in South Dakota. We lived a few miles from Sturgis, the biker capital of the world. Dad bought a little Harley Sportster and would strap a small half-helmet on me, though he never wore one himself. He'd get up on the bike and push aside the kickstand and tell me to climb up and be careful of the exhaust pipe. I'd climb aboard and he'd rev the engine and take off and sometimes we'd just take ourselves around the block. Other times, when Mom was tucked away in bed in one of her moods, he'd take me out into the hills where we'd wind around amidst the green trees and cliffs, just spending the time together without saying a word. We couldn't say a word, of course, because the engine rumbled and the wind slapped at our ears. Probably as close as I'd come in recent memory to the cuddle-fests we had when I was little.

Now, I climbed on the back of Cecilia's father's motorcycle and put on a helmet, as did Cecilia. We putted out the garage door toward the hospital. While my dad's Harley had rumbled with a deep bass roar, this little bike sounded more like a weed-whacker or a lawnmower, but it still felt like we were moving fast.

"Wrap your hands around me, not the seat. It's safer," she yelled over the engine.

I didn't know why I had grabbed the little handles on the seat instead of wrapping my arms around Cecilia; Dad had taught me the same thing. But when I did wrap my arms around her, I have to admit, it didn't feel as safe as it did with Dad. Cecilia was tinier than I thought. I could wrap both arms totally around her without any problem. I felt safer with Dad even though I couldn't get my arms all the way around his big chest and belly.

Cecilia wasn't nearly as good with a bike as Dad, either. She zoomed about and the whole thing shook while going around corners. And then, as we neared the hospital, about a block away actually, she started up from a stop sign and the engine conked out on her and she basically started to lose her balance and her and me and the bike just kinda tipped over very slowly to the side, though we both caught ourselves before landing on the ground.

"Hop off," she told me as she tried to kick start it back to life, but it didn't want to cooperate.

"Here," I said. "Let me try."

She moved to the side and I tried kickstarting the damn thing, but had no better luck. It didn't even come close. On my fifth or sixth attempt, the kickstarter sprung up and slapped me in the back of the foot right in that little thin line of tendon or muscle or whatever it is that runs up to your calf from your heel. I screamed loudly as I felt a burning sensation move up my leg.

"What did you do?"

"I didn't do anything. This damn bike just about broke my ankle." I grabbed the back of my foot.

"That's not your ankle. That's your Achilles tendon, also known as the calcaneal tendon or the tendo calcaneus."

"And this is my foot kicking over this damn bike." I stepped from the motorcycle, let go with my hands, and kicked at the thing. Even though I missed with my kick, the bike fell over from gravity alone. As it landed, the side mirror slapped the pavement and glass shattered in several sharp pieces.

I stormed off toward the hospital with my tendo calcaneus

killing me, my arm slowly dripping blood, and my best friend bent over by the side of the road trying to lift her father's broken bike up off the ground.

The ER nurse deemed my injury nothing to hurry up about, but the cops didn't show up either, so I figured everything would be okay. I thumbed through a copy of Newsweek where the front-page article was about the growing Freedom and Liberty movement. I read how there had been a riot in Seattle when one gang of Freedom and Liberty activists were calling for the state of Washington to round up undocumented workers and send them home. A counterprotest of progressive types got out of hand and the two groups clashed at some community college there. In Chicago, some fringe organization with ties to the Freedom and Liberty Party had begun acting in the middle of the night: breaking out bank windows, spray-painting the sides of buildings, pouring sugar in the gas tanks of police vehicles. A man in New York state drove by a local Home Depot and opened fire with a submachine gun on a group of immigrant day laborers who'd gathered in the parking lot seeding work.

According to the article, police across the country were on alert and stocking up on riot gear and doing trainings on dealing with such things. Apparently, mass demonstrations in these numbers were unheard of since the 1960s and the Vietnam and civil rights protests. The federal government was aiding local jurisdictions with training on dealing with these issues because they were particularly concerned about the major difference between this era and the '60s. While the '60s were primarily protests involving organized groups against the government itself, today's protests were more akin to a civil war. The Freedom and Liberty Party was not a cohesive organization with a solid chain of command and centralized leadership. The Freedom and Liberty Party was more like a gathering of hyenas and buzzards and flies and maggots who'd all come to feast on the same carcass.

Not to mention there was a growing movement of fringe groups on the left as well. Both factions started their battles as a means of swaying government and public opinion, but the centrist government found itself unable to play mediator. It was relegated to a spectator role in a war against two different factions of the

American people, and often state and municipal governments were on one side or the other as well, leaving the feds with little support.

Newsweek quoted an unnamed administration source as saying this was the closest we'd come in over a hundred years to a civil war, and the president was bringing all available resources to bear on the situation because he saw it as a ticking bomb. Only a matter of time before the violence escalated and more people were hurt or killed.

I began thinking about Dad and worrying. He'd never had an audience bigger than a couple of drunk friends and now he was becoming some sort of leader of one of these fringe groups.

As for Cecilia's father, he was politically opposite my dad and he didn't seem like the violent type. At least not back when I read the article in Newsweek. Plus, as far as I could tell, he still hung out with Dad and didn't belong to any progressive/liberal/vegetarian group.

As I sat at the hospital waiting my turn, Cecilia entered with an apologetic smile and I couldn't help but forgive her before she even said a word.

"What're you reading?"

"Check this out … it's fascinating."

Before I could give her a synopsis, a nurse called my name and I left Cecilia with the magazine to get my arm taken care of. In a little room, a friendly doctor took a look at the gash in my arm, and then explained what he'd have to do to stitch it up. A few minutes later he returned, shot my arm up full of Novocaine or some kind of somethingcaine that made it numb. I looked away as I felt the strange sensation of my skin being tugged this way and that while he sewed me up.

To keep my mind off the oddness of the feeling—the pushing and spreading and pulling—I thought about Cecilia out there in the waiting area reading the article I'd just read. I tried to imagine what she thought about it. I tried to imagine how something like that might affect her.

I could never have imagined the depths to which it did.

CHAPTER 21

Band practice went well over the following weeks. Ian slid into our lives and fit the way my fat fingers were learning to slide over the guitar strings. We weren't any sort of boyfriend/girlfriend yet, but the flirting started to get pretty intense. Sometimes after leaving Cecilia's garage, we'd wrestle around on the walk home. This was the start of a new era in which I still saw Cecilia every day, but I was always with Ian when I did. I actually spent more time with him alone than I spent alone with Cecilia. Finally, one day after school, I was early for band practice and Ian was running behind, so Cecilia and I actually had a chance to talk for a change.

"Are you two doing it yet?"

"Cecilia! I can't believe you'd ask something like that. Of course we're not doing it."

"Has he at least kissed you?"

"No, I mean we just kinda sorta wrestle around some. That's pretty much it."

"What do you mean? He wrestles you to the ground?"

"No … I mean, sort of sometimes. I chased after him once and jumped on his back and he flung me around and we ended up rolling around in Mrs. Blaisdell's grass."

"Oh my God. Cecilia! You need to make a move. Ian's obviously too shy to do it himself so you're going to have to help him along."

"What kind of move?"

"Next time you wrestle around with him, jump up before he does and just reach down to give him a hand standing up. Then, when he's standing, don't let go of his hand. I promise you'll be walking with him holding his hand from that point on. Then, you're only one step away from a kiss."

"You think that would really work?"

"Sure. And then, after a few days of hand-holding, you let him walk you to your aunt's front door and you don't let go of his hand when he turns to leave. Instead, you turn to face him and you grab his other hand too and then you get really quiet and stare at his eyes and look down at his lips, and then look back into his eyes and lean in just a little bit. As you lean in, close your eyes extremely slowly like you're really very tired. So tired that you're about to fall asleep. Turn your head a little bit as you do it and … BAM! You'll be kissing."

"Yeah. Sure. I'm just sure that kinda crap will work."

And it did.

That night after band practice, I followed Cecilia's advice to a T and we were standing there on my aunt's porch kissing until the door opened and she cleared her throat and Ian blushed crimson before turning to leave.

After dinner that night Aunt Jennifer asked me if I'd ever had the talk with my mom about the birds and the bees and I assured her that I had, though, of course I never did. Still, I sure as heck didn't want to hear about it from her.

That evening as my head hit the pillow, I found that I couldn't fall asleep for all the thoughts that were running through my head about Ian. I replayed the whole afternoon and the handholding and the kiss over and over again in my head. I thought about how I might have held his hand a little too hard when I helped him off the ground and how I fumbled a little on the porch when I reached for his other hand.

I didn't want to come across as some sort of an aggressive slut, and I swore to myself that tomorrow I'd let him make the moves. If he wanted to. I wasn't going to force anything on him again. After all, he must have gotten the hint with all that we'd gotten up to today.

I started to think about other things that he'd done that afternoon.

How Cecilia had asked me to get her a glass of water while I went into the house to use the bathroom. I started to think that maybe she'd asked me to do it in order to have some time alone with Ian to give him a heads-up about the kissing advice she gave me. Maybe she prodded him a little too.

And then, probably just because it was getting so late, my mind started to worry about things. I started to worry that maybe Cecilia had asked me to get some water so she had alone time with Ian so she could start making some moves on him. I began to think that he was so eager to kiss me because he'd already gotten himself all worked up by kissing Cecilia.

Then I began to worry that maybe this was all some setup. Maybe Cecilia was really a lesbian or a bisexual and she was trying to put together a thing with the three of us. Like I said, I was really tired and my thoughts probably bordered on hallucinations. But I can honestly say that in the middle of the night like that, it seemed like this was all true. I can't explain it other than to say that I felt like it was true.

The next morning I awoke with a horrible, dull ache in the pit of my stomach. It seemed like the dreams or hallucinations or thoughts or whatever they were had moved in the middle of the night from my brain to my gut.

I didn't feel like getting out of bed so I simply didn't.

At some point, Aunt Jennifer came in to prod me toward school, but I told her I was sick and I'm pretty sure it was the green look on my face that convinced her I was telling the truth. She didn't even try to argue with me.

I vaguely remember falling back to sleep and curling up in a tight ball under the covers. I remember pulling the quilt tight around my head so that I could barely breathe. I remember waking up off and on throughout the day and sweating and thinking that maybe I was truly sick. And I remember going back to sleep and tucking myself in again like a caterpillar in a cocoon.

I remember hearing a knock at the door in the afternoon and then hearing Cecilia and Ian's voices calling for me, but I just ignored them and pulled the quilt tighter over my head. I felt nauseous again when the knocking stopped and the calling out for me stopped. They would probably go back to the garage themselves and do it. If they hadn't already been doing it before, they'd probably start now, but I didn't care because I just wasn't up for a fight. Sure, I liked Ian and all, but it wasn't like he was some true love of mine or anything and I didn't feel like getting involved in any sort of a love triangle. Screw that.

Aunt Jennifer came home and asked me how I was feeling and gave me a note that Ian and Cecilia had left on the door for me.

It was written in Ian's handwriting and said simply: Is everything alright?

I just curled back up into a ball in my tight cocoon and tried to sleep. But then, I was screwed because I couldn't sleep at all. I'd slept all day and now it was night and I just lay in bed awake letting all those invasive thoughts pick away at my brain again. Aunt Jennifer stopped by with tomato soup that I could barely eat and some juice that I could barely drink. I lay there awake until midnight or so—long after my aunt went to bed. And then I couldn't sleep, but I was tired of just laying around.

I got up out of my bed and thumbed through a couple books that I had lying around, but none of them really interested me. I tried to read through one, but it was like my eyes were reading over the words and my fingers were turning the pages and I had no idea what I'd just read. I've heard of doing that—spacing off like that—while watching TV, but who knew that a person could read without really reading.

That's when I decided I had to get out of the damn house. I felt jittery and raw and I really had to get out and do something. I could hear the heavy rain slapping against the roof, but I didn't care. And I didn't care that it was past midnight.

I put on a rain jacket and the closest thing I could find that resembled a rain hat. I lifted the bedroom window, but had a hard time getting the screen out. There were these two little tabs but when I pulled on them, all they seemed to do was bend the aluminum frame. I let it bend enough that it came out of the window and then I put it over in my closet where Aunt Jennifer couldn't see it if she peeked in my room in the middle of the night. I doubted that she would, though just in case, I also stuffed a bunch of clothes under my quilt and made it look like a sleeping body.

Once out my window, I started walking along the dark street and let the crisp night air tickle my cheeks. I loved the feeling of being outside the house. I loved how still the world was at that time of night. It was obvious that nobody in this sleepy little corner of the world was awake. There were very few lights on in the houses and no cars driving on the streets. I walked for blocks and never once had to duck behind a tree because of headlights.

I wandered over toward Cecilia's house and saw a light on. Her dad's bedroom was lit up. I could faintly hear the sound of music coming through his slightly open window. It was a song I'd heard before. A singer I'd heard before.

It was my aunt singing "Amazing Grace."

Cecilia must have "borrowed" the tape.

I got closer and peered through the window and saw and odd sight. Cecilia and her father stood in the middle of the room dancing to the sound of my aunt's voice. They swayed back and forth and Cecilia sang along with my aunt. Her father rested his chin on her head.

I stared in awe until the song ended and Cecilia's father kissed her on the forehead and she left the room and headed to her own.

I felt strange and sad and happy all at once. It was hard to explain.

It wasn't exactly creepy—not creepy like there was some sort of funny business going on between them. Creepy like all they had was each other. I know that I complain a lot about my mom and how she's never there, but the truth is that she is there. She's there more than Cecilia's mom, anyway. So when I watched them dance it felt … well … it felt like something special just between them. Something I shouldn't be seeing.

I continued on and when I got near the Mr. Crenshaw, the perv/creeper/Sunday-night-church-collection-plate-guard's house, I was suddenly snapped out of my malaise by a surprise. The curtains of his front window were open wide, though I couldn't recall anytime ever before that he'd had them open like that. So I walked into the yard just far enough to see what was going on. To see if the old perv was molesting somebody. Only, when I got close enough to see what was going on I saw him sitting there on the sofa laughing with some old woman. And as I got closer still, I saw that he was grabbing her or tickling her or something. And when I finally got close enough to make out what was going on, I saw that the old lady on the sofa with the Mr. Crenshaw was someone I knew.

It turned out that the only person the old guy was molesting was my Aunt Jennifer.

CHAPTER 22

It took me awhile to recover from seeing all that. My aunt was hooking up with Mr. Crenshaw on the sly. Must have met him at church. She'd probably been heading over to his house as soon as she thought I was asleep. Now I truly needed to walk along and clear my head.

She couldn't have known him for that long since you'd think he'd have visited her at the hospital. Maybe the knock on her head jarred some sort of common sense loose. But, then I thought about it and remembered that I didn't really have anything against the real Mr. Crenshaw. Just the crazy perv Mr. Crenshaw that I'd made up in my mind.

When I was another block into my walk, a feeling washed over me that I didn't know quite how to describe. It wasn't the first time I'd felt it, but I'd never felt it so strongly. It was the kind of feeling that starts out down low. Maybe even lower than a person's gut. It started out down there somewhere in my bowels, I suppose you'd say. The feeling was like a gurgling, only it wasn't real. The feeling was more like a ghost gurgling. And it gurgled up into my stomach and then up through my chest. It felt as if bubbles were frothing up through my body and replacing all of my organs—replacing anything solid with thin filmy bubbles filled with nothing.

And it continued to rise up into my throat where, again, it strangled out anything solid and left nothingness in its wake. Don't get me wrong; this wasn't a physical sensation. This was a spiritual sensation. I felt as if there were two of me—the physical me and something … I suppose you could call it a soul, but I don't really like that word. There was the me that existed on this planet and the me that existed even when I couldn't feel the physical me anymore.

So, this other me—the soul part, for lack of a better term—was filling up with bubbles and they were moving up inside me, starting from my bowels. The bubbles raised into my throat and then into my brain and I felt like I had a head full of cotton candy and that's where I was walking on a deserted street corner and feeling, well, feeling nothing in a way.

That was the best description of the feeling. It was an anti-feeling. It was the lack of feeling. I didn't feel mad or sad or scared or happy or, or ... anything.

I suppose I did feel alone.

Alone.

That was what the anti-feeling was all about.

Lonesome.

That was a better term. Better than alone or loneliness.

When I was a little kid and my grandma died, I wrote a Christmas card to my grandpa. In the card I asked him how he was feeling. That wasn't my dad's idea or my mom's idea. Simply my idea. It was the kind of thing a person should ask a grandpa when your grandma had just died.

He took the time to write me back and I remember that he wrote in this scratchy writing that looked exactly how you'd expect an old person to write. Like maybe his hand was shaking when he did it. But I also knew that his handwriting was shaky because my Grandpa had lost his right arm in a corn-picker accident when he was a teenager. Before that he'd been right-handed. I once heard that ever since the corn-picker accident, his handwriting had been pretty sketchy. I remember being told that by Dad, but I'm not sure that I'd ever actually seen his handwriting.

Anyway, the thing he wrote was this:

Hi Olivia,

Thanks for writing and Merry Christmas to you as well. I'm doing alright. Just feeling a little lonesome.

And that basically summed it up for me. This feeling. It came about every few years and it always caught me by surprise. It felt a lot like when the dentist makes you inhale laughing gas or the way it feels when you spin in a circle until you get so dizzy that you're

114

ready to fall. Only instead of lasting only a few seconds, it lasts weeks. It lasts so long that you barely remember when it started and you barely notice when it ended.

Only this time I did notice when it started. It started after I saw Cecilia with her father and Aunt Jennifer with the perv—I mean Mr. Crenshaw. It started while I was out wandering through the night.

And this time the feeling had a name:

Lonesome.

CHAPTER 23

Believe it or not, our band started sounding good.

I don't even know when it happened, but a few weeks into practicing and Ian had taught me the three chords he said I needed to know, and he was drumming, and Cecilia was singing, and we were simply trying to get down one song and when we got it down one day and played it all the way through without any screwups it suddenly clicked in my mind that we truly were a band.

"Holy crap!" I said.

"I think we did it," Cecilia added.

"Not bad. All we need is a few more songs and we'll be ready to perform out in public. My buddy Byrd has a band that's playing at the mall at the game shop there. He'd let us open for them."

"What next?" I asked. "You have any more original songs?"

"I have tons," Ian answered, but Cecilia interrupted him.

"There's a cover song I really want to do."

And I knew before she went any further exactly what it was, though Ian grinned and guessed something totally different as he broke into a version of the Simon & Garfunkel tune: "...Ceciiiilia, you're breakin' my heart. You're shakin' my confidence daily. Ohhh Ceciiiilia, I'm down on my knees. I'm beggin' you please to come home. Come on home..."

And he stood up from behind his drum kit and jumped out front with Cecilia and grabbed her hand and started swinging her around while making "boom boom" sounds with his mouth. After the second or third spin, they sang it together. I have to admit that my gut knotted up.

"Makin' love in the afternoon with Cecilia, up in my bedroom..."

And then Cecilia chimed in with another "Makin' looove."

And I felt like I was about to throw up.

They went on like this for quite awhile—singing and spinning and even though they were the ones doing it, I was the one that started feeling dizzy and sick to my stomach. Ian spun her out into the middle of the garage while still holding her hand, then he'd spin her back into his arms again and they'd grin and look into one another's eyes like they were in love or something. Besides the spinning stomach, I started to feel very warm like I was getting some sort of a fever. And then I could barely breathe as I sat there watching them all dancing around and making googly eyes at each other.

"I'll be right back," I told them in the middle of a pirouette.

I think I was reasonably calm when I said it. Said it like I just had to run off to the bathroom or something. But the minute I got out of the garage, I simply had to keep walking. I was having the nightmare thoughts all over again. I knew that it shouldn't bother me so much, but I couldn't help myself. I mean, if they were actually getting it on in secret or something, would they be doing all that right in front of me?

I decided to tough it out and come back to the garage. As I neared the door, I have to admit that I half expected to find Cecilia stretched out over Ian's drum kit or something with him going at her. Instead, the two of them were simply standing by the keyboard and Cecilia had dragged out an old tape deck and was playing my aunt's version of "Amazing Grace."

They stood in silent reverie listening to Aunt Jennifer's voice. Ian looked up and smiled at me while Cecilia glanced my direction. She quickly looked back to the tape with what appeared to be tears in her eyes. For some reason, Cecilia's crying got to me too and I felt myself tearing up. I don't know if it was just the song or the song and Ian or the song and Ian and my best friend all standing there hearing my aunt's powerful voice belting out the music.

Whatever it was, none of us spoke until the song was over and we could hear only the scratchy hiss of the old tape.

"Wow. She has incredible range," Ian said.

Cecilia and I nodded, though I don't know for sure if either of us knew what he meant. I supposed that Cecilia probably did, though.

Ian grabbed some blank sheet music, rewound the tape, and began writing down what he heard. He hit the pause button every few seconds and caught up, then hit play again, never needing to rewind. He looked like the focused, crazed version of Mozart that I'd once seen in the old movie Amadeus. When Ian had totally finished, he finally hit the rewind button and then played the whole thing through again to double-check his notations.

During the whole six minutes or so, Cecilia and I just stood and watched.

"Looks like I got it," he said. "Let me show you two what all this means."

And he went on to explain stuff like Every Good Boy Does Fine and Every Good Boy Deserves Fudge and all kinds of nifty tricks like that, though I got so caught up in his mastery that I barely paid attention to the learning.

I stared at him the whole time he explained it, while Cecilia stared at the sheet music and soaked it all in. In a way, I felt like a dork, just staring all longingly at Ian like that, but I also felt as if I couldn't help myself. I was totally in love and there seemed to be no getting out of it. At the end of rehearsal, Cecilia promised that she would practice what he showed her and I knew that she would.

On the walk home that day, Ian and I didn't wrestle at all, but we only made it about a block home before I took his hand in mine and stopped walking and turned toward him.

"What's up?"

"You're pretty good, huh?"

"What do you mean?" he asked.

"Just what I said. But let me ask you a question."

"Shoot."

"Do you like Cecilia the same way you like me?"

Ian laughed and shook his head. "Are you kidding me?"

"Just curious."

"I mean Cecilia is cute and all, but c'mon. She's such a Goody Two-Shoes."

I immediately thought about the musical equipment and all the ways that I knew perfectly well that Cecilia was not a Goody

Two-Shoes. Besides which, Ian had seen her do some bad things too.

"Are you forgetting who bounced that gum off that lady's boob?"

"Oh, come on, Olivia. She was just showing off to you. You're like her hero."

I was struck dumb at the notion. Me? Cecilia's hero?

"Are you high?"

"What do you mean?"

"You think I'm Cecilia's hero? That girl's only hero is herself."

"Yeah, right." He rolled his eyes.

I realized that he was totally serious.

"Why in the world would you think that about her? All she ever does is lecture me on how to be a better person. She treats me like I'm some sort of disease that needs to be cured."

Ian stopped and turned to me with a big grin. "Sometimes I forget that you've led a kind of sheltered life."

"Me? A sheltered life? Dude, I've been halfway around the country more times than you've probably left Urbandale. I've seen and done things that would ..."

"Whoa. Whoa. You're making my point for me. Why do you think Cecilia looks up to you so much? I'm just saying that you've lived a kinda sheltered life by not having parents that are constantly explaining this kinda stuff to you. Cecilia is simply acting out when she gives you her little lectures. She's compensating for her own lack of self-confidence. You should see the way she looks at you. She studies you. She wants to be you."

Though the words were clear enough, this made no sense to me. On some intellectual level, I totally understood what he was saying. My right brain or left brain, or whatever part of my brain that was logical had one of those "Aha!" moments that I imagine scientists get in the lab before their work takes them in a new direction. The other side of my brain, however, was twisted into an orb of confusion. I felt like a kitten clawing at a ball of yarn and unraveling it throughout the house trying to get to the middle and discover if there was some sort of catnip in there somewhere. And, after standing slack-jawed for awhile I discovered just how apt my catnip metaphor really was. I felt high from the revelation.

I felt ecstatic. Inside, I was purring and rolling and mewing.

Cecilia looked up to me!

"That's it, Ian. That's it."

"What's it?"

"I had no clue, and now I'm clued in. Everything makes sense now."

I threw my arms around his neck and planted a huge kiss on his lips. And when I found his lips responding to mine, I took it a step further and opened my mouth like I was going to swallow him whole. We made out like that for what seemed like twenty minutes about a block from my aunt's house. And then Ian got a little cocky and let his hand slide down my back to the top of my butt. He let his fingers slip under the waistband of my jeans and I laughed and put my hand on his chest.

"Whoa there, Mickey Mouse. My body is not a ride at Disneyland."

I laughed when I said it, but I could tell that Ian was totally embarrassed. His hand froze and he backed off two steps and blushed. "I'm ... mmmm ... sorry Olivia ... I ... ummm ..."

"Geez, Ian, who lived the sheltered life now? I'm not yelling rape at the top of my lungs or anything. Just slowing you down a little when we're so close to my aunt's house."

His blush took a few beats to fade, but I took Ian's hand and I was able to walk the rest of the way home feeling like a sweet youngster instead of a drunk coed at a frat party. Ian's blush totally disappeared by the time we stood on the sidewalk in front of Aunt Jennifer's. That being the case, I decided I should take advantage of the situation and put the blush back on his face.

"Don't I get a goodbye kiss?"

"Um, sure." He said and as he leaned in to give me a peck, I took his right hand, the one that I'd been holding and I brought it up to my chest and I pressed his palm against my left breast. Talk about blushing red. Not only did he blush red, but he pulled his hand away from me like he had just touched a hot stovetop.

"Hey! What do you think? My body's a ride at Disneyland?" he said.

I laughed but not before I looked past Ian's shoulder to see Dad standing there on my aunt's porch with his eyes all scrunched up like he was trying to see something. Of course, what he was trying to see was just exactly where Ian's hand had gotten off to, but I was pretty sure that he couldn't see it.

"Olivia Louise, why don't you come up here and let me meet your friend."

From the tone of his voice, I changed my mind and thought maybe he had seen the whole thing.

Ian was the perfect, polite gentleman as he reached out his hand to shake Dad's. I could tell by the way Dad stared him down that he must have put an iron grip on the handshake. Ian was smart enough not to shake his hand in pain, or anything, though.

"You must be Ian?"

I had no idea anyone knew who Ian was with the exception of Cecilia and myself, but I was about to find out that someone had been doing some serious spying.

CHAPTER 24

My dad shook Ian's hand and acted polite enough to him. I was a little worried, though. We'd never much talked about boys, and even though I'd had a few crushes and stuff, I never really dated any guys and wasn't sure just how my dad would react. Unlike other kids, I'd never gotten any sort of a birds and bees talk from either of my parents, and it was just pretty much the kind of thing a person didn't talk about at my house.

And, I know this sounds odd because it's such an obvious thing, but Ian was a black kid and my dad was not too fond of black people. That's not to say he didn't sometimes have black friends himself, but he mostly thought they were out to take something away from him.

"So I hear you're a landscaper, Mr. Driscoll?"

"Actually, kid, I'm a Gardener 2 and don't you forget it." My dad answered as if he was totally serious.

Ian, fortunately, didn't fall for it. "Oh, that sounds much more important than landscaper. When will you graduate to Gardener 3?"

I was honestly shocked that Ian went there. He had guts, but it worked. Dad smiled and slapped him on the back. "I like you, kid. You're spunky. Not that I would have ever imagined Olivia hooking up with some little pussy-boy, though."

I cringed when he said that. Not the pussy-boy part, but the hooking-up part. Did Dad even know what he was saying?

"Anyway, I have to be home for dinner in a few minutes but it was nice to meet you."

And with that Ian left too early. Too early because that meant it was just Dad and me and I didn't know what this visit was all about in the first place. Ian and I did a little awkward hug and that left me standing alone on the porch with Dad.

"What say we go and get a bite to eat?" he asked.

"Actually I think Aunt Jennifer..."

"Naw. Don't worry. I already ran it by her and she said she didn't have anything planned. I was thinking we could head out to Ponderosa and get us a big ol' steak and salad bar."

"Sure."

The drive was quiet, but Dad kept taking his eyes off the road to look over at me. He was a good driver, though, so it didn't cause any problems. No near accidents like we would have had if Mom had been driving. Eventually, as he neared the Ponderosa parking lot, he asked me simple question to which I didn't know the answer.

"So ... how's your life going?"

"Um ... everything's OK."

"Aunt Jennifer said that you started playing in a band with Ian and Cecilia. What kind of music are you playing?"

"I'm not sure. Pretty much just rock 'n' roll. Kind of this alternative rock/ hip-hop thing. We play some old songs too."

"And you're playing guitar? That's awesome."

"Yeah."

We took a breather from talking while we loaded up our plates at the salad bar. I went for a chocolate cream pie with curled dark chocolate on top just to see if Dad would say anything about splurging, but he didn't. Dad got a T-bone and I went for the ground steak, which I knew from past experience was mostly just a juicy, big hamburger.

"How's Mom?"

"Oh, she's doing pretty well."

"Is she doing anything?"

"Believe it or not, she's taking a class."

I was shocked. "What kind of class?"

He laughed before he told me, so I knew it would be a doozy. "It's called Ecstatic Dance. Some sort of hippy-dippy thing that this neighbor lady teaches. A cross between dancing and therapy, as far as I can tell."

"What about you?" I asked, though I knew he wasn't taking

any sort of Ecstatic Dance class. I figured he'd either say something about that Freedom and Liberty Party business or nothing at all. I doubted he'd brag about drinking down at the bar.

"Actually, believe it or not I just got made Chapter President of the Polk County Freedom and Liberty Party."

I could feel my eyebrows crinkling up, even though I tried to keep them in a straight line. "What does that mean?"

"Oh ... I mostly organize mailings and things like that. I'll be organizing a protest on the Capitol in a couple weeks. I guess I just can't stand to see what's happening to this country anymore with all the illegals and the..." He stopped short when he saw the expression on my face. I guess it was pretty obvious that I didn't want to hear any of it. I half figured he was going to say something about the blacks, but thought about Ian and decided to keep his mouth shut.

"Anyway, it gives me something to do after work besides drinking too much." He smiled when he said it, but it was an uneasy smile.

His smile told me a lot. In fact, I had a feeling that was the whole reason he wanted to go out with me. To say that one little line.

"You're not drinking anymore?"

"Oh ... I wouldn't say that. But I've cut down quite a bit."

You'd think I'd be really excited about this, but he'd cut down on drinking before—mostly when we were new to some town. The minute he met up with a group of drinking buddies, that all changed. This did seem different, though, because we weren't new to Urbandale at this point. In fact we were moving in on a record for staying longer than we'd stayed anywhere. This made me a little nervous.

"How's your job going?"

"It's fine. Nothing to write home about, but I can't complain too much either. It's a job."

"What are you doing? Pretty much mowing lawns and stuff?"

"Yeah. Doing some hedge-trimming and minor pruning. Crap like that. I've done worse. And the nice part is that the bosses mostly leave us alone. I get a few hours a day that I can sit in the truck and work on things."

I let that soak in.

"Work on what things?"

"Oh, stuff for the Freedom and Liberty Party mostly."

His voice trailed off when he said that and I could tell that something was a little off about the whole Freedom and Liberty Party thing. I couldn't quite read if Dad was embarrassed about it all or he was trying to keep some sort of a secret about it all. He immediately changed the subject, though, so I knew he wasn't interested in discussing it any more.

"How's school coming along?"

"It's ... well ... it's school."

"Are you actually going?"

"Yeah. I mean I didn't at first, but I am now."

I knew his smile was because of my honesty about it. I guess we'd both come a long way here in Urbandale.

He paused as if he were carefully measuring the next thing he was going to say before saying it. It was a big pause. The sort of pause that usually preceded the announcement of another move across the country. Since things seemed to be going well, though, I feared something even worse. Maybe it was the type of pause that preceded the announcement of a divorce. Maybe someone in the family was dying.

"Just go ahead and tell me what you need to tell me. I can take it."

"I'm not sure what you mean. I don't have anything to tell you. I ... well ... I had a question I wanted to ask you. But nothing to tell you."

"All right. Shoot."

"I'm just wondering how things are going with you and Cecilia. Has she been doing all right lately?"

"Cecilia? Sure. Things are fine."

"Okay. Just wondering."

"Why?"

"Well. I know that sometimes when a girl gets a new boyfriend, she sometimes neglects her friends. I don't want you to neglect Cecilia, though."

"What makes you think I'd neglect her?"

"Oh ... I don't think you would. But I just want to make sure that everything is going all right between the two of you."

The look of concern on his face told me I wasn't getting the whole story.

"What's the deal? Do you know something that I don't know?"

"Well, I just worry about her sometimes. Her dad has been acting a little strange lately and I heard some things and ... I just want to make sure everything is okay in their family."

"What kind of things did you hear?"

I don't know why, but my thoughts immediately went to pervy stuff again. Probably because I'd seen that whole dancing-together thing the other night. But also because it was pretty odd for Dad to be worrying about somebody like this.

"I just heard that maybe Cecilia had been going through some hard times lately. Her father missed some work recently and somebody ... well ... someone at work said they heard that Cecilia had tried to ... um ... tried to hurt herself. Did you ever hear anything like that?"

"Cecilia? Hurt herself? You've got to be kidding. She hasn't missed a day of school. I think she hasn't missed a day of school ever as far as that goes. How do they say she tried to hurt herself?"

"I think it was just a rumor, Ollie. Just a stupid rumor. Don't worry about it."

He called me Ollie when he was trying to placate me, but I wasn't feeling much like being placated. "What are they trying to say? Are they trying to say she like took a bunch of pills or something?"

"Not exactly. But listen. If you haven't noticed anything happening with her, I'm sure it's just some sort of stupid rumor at work. I'm sure there's nothing to it."

"Just tell me, at least. What are they saying?"

"One of the guys at work just said that Cecilia tried to cut her wrists, but obviously if she had you'd be the first one to know. Right? I mean the two of you are still close. You'd know."

"Of course I'd know. That's about the stupidest thing I've ever heard. If Cecilia did anything like that, I'd be the first to know."

"I figured that. Just checking in though, sweetie. I hate to imagine you trying to deal with something big like that without any support from your Mom and Dad."

I just let his last statement hang there in the air in all of its stupidity. I'd dealt with lots of things. Tough, horrible things without any support of anybody. Not to mention, Mom was nowhere to be seen during this conversation anyway.

For the rest of our meal we got off on some tangent about some of the places that we used to live. We discussed Novi and Indiana and Houston. We reminisced like we were a couple of old folks recalling some war or another. But still, in the back of my brain, itching like a bedbug bite, I worried about Cecilia. I worried about why a bunch of guys at Dad's work would be spreading a bunch of lies about her like that.

The next day, I showed up at her house in the morning, just like I did most days before school, but she had left a note on her door that said she'd already left and would meet me at school. It was somewhat odd behavior, but not totally. It wasn't the first time she'd done it. Throughout most of the school day, she seemed to avoid me. We'd run across each other, but she was always in some hurry to get off to somewhere else.

Finally, I caught up with her as the last bell rang and started to walk beside her toward band practice and home, but the minute we got to the parking lot, her dad was sitting out there in his green Urbandale Parks and Rec truck waiting for her.

"C'mon Cecilia. We're going to be late."

"I'm sorry Olivia. I forgot I have a doctor appointment. Tell Ian I'll be a little late, but you two can start without me. The garage is unlocked."

She ran off toward the truck before I could do anything to stop her.

When she finally arrived in the garage, she seemed out of it. Ian went in the house to use the restroom and I figured I'd take the chance to warn her about all the stupid rumors that some yahoos had been spreading about her. I started to broach the subject with an "Oh my god. You won't believe what those nuts at your dad's work have been saying…."

But before I got any further, Cecilia stretched both her arms above her head in some sort of a yoga pose or something and I couldn't miss it.

Her sleeves fell practically to her elbow and exposed a thick bandage around her left wrist.

CHAPTER 25

I didn't finish my statement about the rumor at our dad's work and didn't say a word through the rest of practice. Ian had to leave early because of a private lesson with a piano instructor. He told me he'd swing back by the garage in about an hour, but that left Cecilia and me some time to ourselves.

When Cecilia tried to get me to talk about the gossip, I made up some BS about saying the Parks and Rec were going to lay some people off.

"Well, you know that they do layoffs by seniority. That means your dad would be one of the first to go."

"I know. And I'm afraid if that happened I'd probably be moving again," I said just to stick it to her for being such a pain.

"But what about the band?" she asked, as if that was the only thing that mattered in the world.

"I guess the band would have to break up too. I don't know what you guys would do."

"I suppose we could find another guitarist. I bet Ian has lots of friends who play."

I was really getting sick of this line of discussion, and I was perturbed that all she seemed to care about was the band.

"Actually, I think that Ian would probably quit the band too. He told me once that he would probably quit if I ever did."

Of course, I made all this crap up, but she was really getting on my nerves. She reached lightly brush her right fingers against her bandaged wrist and I suddenly felt that sick to the pit—no—to the core of my stomach feeling again. What the hell was I doing? Why was I messing with her emotions like that when she ... well ... she was obviously in some sort of great pain. I stared into

Cecilia's eyes until I could feel the tears welling up in mine. What was I doing?

"I'm so sorry, Cecilia. I'm so, so sorry."

She stared at me with a curious expression. Something like she was studying me in biology class. Like I was a little pig fetus cut open and displayed for her to investigate. Like my skin was pulled back. Sharp, thin pins jabbed through it into the black, waxy surface of an aluminum tray.

"What's gotten into you?"

"Nothing. I mean ... Cecilia ... I just love you so much and I'm sorry we're fighting like this."

"We're not fighting."

"Well ... I'm sorry that I'm being a jerk. I just want you to know that I love you so much. So, so much."

She stared back into my eyes and a flicker of light danced between us and I began to feel warm toward her. I began to feel the way I'd felt when we first became best friends. I genuinely liked Cecilia and it had been awhile since I'd been able to say that.

"I think we should spend some more time hanging out. Just the two of us," I told her.

"Why? Are you afraid I'm going to steal your boyfriend?"

It took me only a beat to respond, and in that beat I realized just how far I'd come since I moved to this ridiculous little suburban town. A few months ago and I would have knocked the stupid bitch upside the head. Weeks ago and I may have just broken down crying or yelled something along the lines of you idiot, I was trying to save your life. But now, being this far along in this big drama of a life that I found myself in, I shook my head a little and felt sorry for her. I felt sorry because she'd lost her mother and because she always had to act like she was some princess whose crap didn't stink like everyone else. And I felt sorry because she didn't know any better. And I felt sorry because I didn't know any way to make her cry and I think that was all she really needed to do. One big cry and I think she would have been fine. Well, maybe more than one cry, but the girl needed to do some crying.

Hitting Cecilia wouldn't do the trick and I knew that saying something mean about her mother wouldn't do it because she already knew how to put her defenses up about all that.

So, I simply shook my head and pursed my lips and said, "Listen, Cecilia, I'm not afraid of you stealing Ian, but I admit that I used to be. I'm just afraid that you're truly hurting inside and you need some help, but you're not asking for it."

Cecilia stared at me like I hadn't said a thing. Then her eyebrows scrunched together a little bit and she abruptly changed the subject. "We're really getting this band together, huh?"

"Yeah."

"I mean. I think that's a good thing, you know. Like I was saying before about having some purpose to life."

"Yeah. I can see that. I'm not sure I'd call the band the purpose to my life, exactly, but it's fun. Plus, like my dad said, it keeps me out of trouble."

Cecilia smiled. "How are your dad and mom doing anyway?"

"They're good. I haven't talked to Mom in a couple weeks, but it sounds like she's doing things and that's always a sign that she's feeling okay. And, believe it or not, my dad said he hasn't been going out drinking. I'm like totally shocked and I doubt it'll last, but … well … if it's true that's a good thing."

"I know. I heard about that."

"You heard that my dad's not drinking?"

"My father mentioned it to me. He said your dad went all nuts and found a bunch of other nuts and they're all religious and against drinking and against foreigners and stuff."

I didn't say anything.

"And my father also said that your dad was turning into one of those crazies like the guy who drove his plane into that building full of innocent people and killed all the kids at the daycare."

She was looking for some reaction, but I didn't give her one.

"Anyway, that's why I was asking you how your mom and dad were doing because I was worried that they were going crazy and you didn't even know about it, but it sounds more like they're going crazy and you do know about it."

I didn't say anything, but I started to pack up my bag to go.

"I thought you were going to wait for Ian to get back?"

"I think I'll head out and meet Ian halfway."

I could practically hear her heart beating faster as she jumped in front of me and tried to get in my way so I wouldn't leave. She was panicked.

"You don't have to leave right now do you? Or, I could walk with you to meet Ian. I don't think we get enough time together to talk."

"Sure. C'mon and walk with me."

We walked in silence for the most part, but I could feel how much Cecilia needed to be with me and I really wanted to help her in some way. Walking in silence sure as heck beat her making fun of me with little jabs. The silence also gave me a chance to think up a plan for helping her.

Ian met us and immediately began his little flirtations with Cecilia, though by this point I couldn't care less.

"So I see I get two hotties for the price of one today."

Cecilia eked out a slight grin, but I could tell that she wasn't into playing with Ian today. Even though I wasn't jealous, it was probably just as well.

When we got to the corner of Douglas and 85th, I turned right instead of left.

"Where are we going?" Cecilia asked.

"Just follow me."

"What are you up to?" Ian asked.

I ignored him.

And we kept going until we got to the bus stop and then we waited for the next bus.

"C'mon." I said as the bus stopped and let out a high hiss of air before the doors opened to what would be our last—well, second-to-last adventure together.

CHAPTER 26

The Imperial Lanes was clear on the other side of Des Moines. The three of us approached the double glass doors cautiously, as though we knew we were in for something foreign.

An old man stood outside by an ashtray. He alternately smoked a cigarette and coughed up a lung or two. His skin was the color and texture of an old tangerine that I once found behind my dresser when we moved from Knightdale, North Carolina to Snelleville, Georgia. The old man had one eye that seemed to follow us and another eye that looked down at the cigarette that dangled from his mouth. He would inhale and then let the smoke blow out his nose and curl up into the air toward the bad eye. As far as I could tell, none of us looked toward his face as we passed, but the minute we got into the door, our faces stared at one another and Cecilia broke the silence and seemed, at the same time, to break her mood.

"Oh my god!" she said and all three of us broke into fits of laughter.

By the time we got to the counter, the old lady sitting there was giving us a dirty look. Probably expecting that we were up to no good, though I don't know how three kids who decided to spend time at a bowling alley could be up to anything but good. This was the closest thing to being good that I'd done in a long time.

"We would like to do bowling," Ian said with a smirk because he knew perfectly well that nobody does bowling.

"Just a minute," the old lady said. Her smoky Listerine breath practically bowled us over. "LOU!"

"LOU!" she yelled for a second time and the old man we'd

seen outside followed her screech and joined her behind the counter.

"I don't actually work here," she told us as she settled back onto her stool.

The old guy looked at me and said, "Five?"

"No, just the three of us."

"I mean size five?"

I had no idea what in the world the dude was talking about.

"Your shoes? Size five?"

I know that I must have looked like a total idiot standing there staring at his good eye, but I was clueless. Shoes? But then it hit me: bowling shoes. I wasn't a bowler, but I knew enough to realize that you need bowling shoes to go bowling. They were slick on the bottom so you could slide across the floor.

"Yeah. Five."

He guessed Cecilia and Ian's shoe sizes as well and pointed out the racks of balls and told us we'd be in lane one. Everyone else who was bowling that day was at the other end of the building in lanes 14 through 22.

There was something very comforting about the sound and smell of a bowling alley. It smelled … well … new, for lack of a better word. And the constant sounds of balls rolling and pins exploding and people chatting took us out of the dull, humdrum lives that we lived day to day. I know it sounds odd to consider being a teenager and playing in a band and stealing things and all the other crap we were up to as being boring and consider bowling to be exciting, but it was. I suppose that was because we were all three a little nervous down there at the end of the building by ourselves with all these other folks drinking and yucking it up. And the lazy-eyed, chain-smoking owner, and the crazy old woman that worked behind the counter but didn't really work there.

It was just the recipe we needed to shine a little light in Cecilia's life.

From her first gutterball in the first frame to her third strike in the tenth, she started to come alive. Well … maybe not so much come alive, but she wasn't quite so … I was going to say dead, but I'm getting caught up a little on the word. I'm feeling flush and a little nauseous. But I'll just say that she certainly acted more excited about things than I'd seen her be in months.

Ian had a good time too, though Ian had a good time with anything he did. He rolled more gutter balls than either of us, but he also threw the ball halfway down the lane and it always bounced a couple of times before hitting the gutter or crashing into the pins. I made a note to myself to keep an eye on Ian for some unresolved anger issues.

"I think I pretty much beat both of you, but I'm up for another game if you are," Cecilia said with a grin.

I'd gotten used to Cecilia's unrelenting attitude of being better than everyone. Funny thing was that I had a vague recollection of thinking that about her when I first met her, and then giving her the benefit of the doubt. Now, I think I really understood her and saw that it was all just a defense mechanism. It really didn't bother me anymore. And it wasn't just because I understood why she did it. I also felt better about myself lately so I was less likely to think she really was better than me.

Ian never felt less than anyone, so it hadn't been an issue for him.

"Sure, let's go again," he said.

"Maybe this time you can launch the ball all the way to the pins without messing with the floor at all." Cecilia said.

I laughed and Ian said he'd try, which he did.

Somehow, and I'm not even sure myself how I managed it, I won the second game, which left Cecilia in a bit of a funk. Since I'd schemed all of this as a way to brighten her mood, I purposely tried to bowl like crap on the third game. Unfortunately it seemed like Ian and Cecilia were doing the same thing. Going into the fourth frame I had something like 13 and Cecilia and Ian were still in single digits.

I could tell Cecelia was getting tired and figured it was directly related to her losing. So I tried even harder to throw the game which had my ball heading into the gutter practically the second it was out of my hands.

Ian was throwing the ball in a high arc so that it now only managed about two bounces before hitting the pins. When he did that in the seventh frame, the old man with the bad eye approached us from behind and cleared his throat.

"I think that you three are done for the day."

"What?" Cecilia asked.

"I said that the three of you are done for the day. Please turn in your shoes and you can come up and pay for the three games you bowled."

"But we didn't finish the third game. We still have two frames to go," Cecilia said.

"I said you're done for the day."

That one simple statement by an old man with orange-peel skin seemed to erase all the progress I'd made with Cecilia over the afternoon. I could see the blood boiling up inside of her. Her pot of tomato soup ready to boil over. The lid was clambering up and down. Chattering as the steam got hotter and hotter.

"We're not paying for the third game unless you let us finish it."

The old man seemed to stare at her as if truly weighing his options. He ignored her and instead turned to Ian: "If you bounce that ball one more time I'm charging you extra for damage to the lanes."

"I'm really sorry about that."

"Two more frames."

And he walked away to let us finish.

Ian spread his legs and rolled the ball slowly with both hands and grinned at Cecilia and me as it trickled down the lane.

I was next and I somehow managed to throw a strike.

And then, Cecilia got up to bowl and she heaved the ball as high in the air as she could manage and in the split second before I realized what was happening, I ran a little dream sequence through my head. I imagined the ball bouncing down the alley and I imagined Cecilia telling the old guy "You told him not to bounce it, but you didn't tell me." And I imagined the guy kicking us out or holding us hostage and calling our parents. I imagined all kinds of things in that split second, though they all revolved around the idea of the ball bouncing down the alley.

Instead, though, Cecilia had lofted the ball so high that it smashed into the flat-screen monitor above her head—the one that showed our scores. The monitor shattered into hundreds of glass and plastic pieces and rained down on Cecilia's head even as the bowling ball itself fell to the earth aimed at my friend.

She looked up and saw it headed her way and ducked just as it thudded against the side of her arm and all three of us ran through the emergency exit, not knowing how close behind us the old man was.

We slipped and slid the whole way home in our bowling shoes.

CHAPTER 27

That was the last time we had any fun with Cecilia. I'm pretty sure about that, though there were still a few weeks before she died.

The band practiced and we got better. Besides our first original and a cover of Aunt Jennifer's song, we also did a cover of "Cecilia" by Simon and Garfunkel, and tucked a few more of Ian's originals under our belt. Practice was fun and I really thought things were getting better for my friend. The weird thing was that she seemed less depressed as she came close to the end. She actually seemed to perk up a bit on the days right before she did it.

Dad was getting totally serious about all this Freedom and Liberty Party business. I heard from my aunt that he was going to organizing meetings four or five nights a week. He even started to swing by the house and say hi to me after his meetings. It was one of the best periods of time I ever spent with Dad. He'd show up at the house—completely sober, mind you—and he'd hang out with me and my aunt. At first he'd just sit in front of the TV next to us, but after several days of that routine, my aunt asked if he wanted to play some cards and we'd all move into the kitchen and play poker or blackjack and talk about our day.

"I hear that band of yours is really coming along."

"From Cecilia's dad?"

"Yeah. He mentioned it at work the other day. Said sometimes he walks past the garage and thinks you're playing a stereo in there or something."

I was surprised to hear that Mr. French would say anything like that.

"He told me you guys are ready to go play out somewhere."

"Maybe. Ian may have lined up an opening for us at the mall

for this thing. He has other friends in other bands."

"That's great. I'm very proud of you, Olivia."

I felt my face scrunch up as if to ward off the compliment, but I stopped myself and figured, what the hell, I deserve it. The blood rushed into my cheeks and realized I was blushing. I wasn't a blusher, and my dad knew that too and that made him do a little blushing himself.

I think my aunt noticed our discomfort, and came to the rescue and changed the subject.

"So, how's Marie doing?"

A couple funny things happened when Aunt Jennifer asked that. First thing I thought was, who the hell is Marie? Then I realized that Marie was my mom and, of course, I knew that perfectly well. But I wasn't used to anyone calling her Marie and also I actually hadn't done much thinking about her lately. I know that seems cold or hard-hearted or something, but we really didn't have much in common and I barely ever saw her during this time. The other funny thing was that I felt my heart racing a bit because, well, Dad generally wasn't interested in talking about how she was doing. But, again, I was surprised by his response.

"She's doing great. Going to her Ecstatic Dance thing on Saturday's now and she found this group of women that she meets with on Tuesday nights to get together and talk about life or something with. Sort of an offshoot of the Ecstatic Dancers. They call it the Gathering and they sometimes read books together and they sometimes just talk from what I understand."

I could see my aunt's eyebrows raise the way they do when she's pleasantly surprised about something.

"Full house," Dad said and we pushed the pile of pennies toward him.

He was way better at poker than Aunt Jennifer or me. Somehow I was even proud of that fact about him lately. If you'd have asked me a year ago, I would have been embarrassed that he was so good at poker. He was only good at it because he spent so many hours wasted and away from home with his buddies. But now, it was like everything else about him. Like the Freedom and Liberty Party thing. He somehow managed to turn his crazy ranting about the government into something that was … was …

for lack of a better word, constructive.

Not that I agreed with anything they stood for. They were all crazy, nuts, but at least now he was a crazy guy who wasn't drunk all the time and he'd found friends who didn't think he was crazy.

"How's it going with you and Ian?" Dad asked with a combination sneer/grin.

"Oh, Reggie. That is none of your business," Aunt Jennifer said.

"I'm just asking. Wanting to make sure he's treating my little girl well."

"He treats me well. You think I'd let anyone treat me anything but well?"

Dad and Aunt Jennifer laughed at that, though I actually hadn't meant it to be very funny.

"But he's going off to college in a couple months. Are you two going to have a long-distance relationship?" he asked.

"We don't think like that right now. Who knows, though."

"I guess it won't be long until you start thinking about college," Dad said.

Aunt Jennifer chimed in again: "She's taking a full load this quarter, you know. Perfect attendance and straight A's."

I blushed.

"I'm taking easy classes is all."

Dad looked at me and I could practically see the chill move up inside him. He held his gaze longer than he had probably ever done in his life. He stared at me and smiled a sad smile, and then turned to my aunt and smiled an even sadder smile. I say "sad," but that's not exactly the right word. He stared at my aunt and his eyes watered and a tear gathered up in the corner of his left eye and it hung there forever. It got so big it looked like a water balloon about ready to burst.

Eventually, it slid down his cheek and caught on sections of his scraggly beard as it made its way to his sharp chin before falling to the ground.

Because I felt uncomfortable in such a sappy moment, a joke came to my mind, though I wasn't about to say it. The joke I thought of was how the tear didn't have far to fall—you know, because of the short thing. My dad, the crying leprechaun. My dad, with a strange version of Short Man Syndrome where he got all sad because of his height instead of getting all angry.

Like I said, I obviously didn't make that joke though I was thinking about it so I wouldn't cry myself. As Dad's tear fell, he quietly turned to my aunt and said, "Thank you for watching after her."

CHAPTER 28

My gut knotted up on the day that Ian came to band practice and told us he'd found us our first gig. Actually, it just got a little queasy when he told us that. The real knots started when he told us where and what.

"Remember my friend in that band Capcha Flag? They're playing a counter-protest at the Capitol next weekend and they hooked us up to open the show."

"What counter-protest?" I asked, though I already knew. It could only be one thing.

"You know, against the Freedom and Liberty Party."

"Really? The two protests are going on at the same time?"

"The Freedom and Liberty Party have the Capitol steps, but we've got the place by the war memorial, so we're only a few hundred feet away."

"Why would a band like us play at a protest?"

"Counter-protest," Ian said. "Because, it's an all-day thing and there'll be speakers and bands and all kinds of things."

"We should bring riot gear," Cecilia said in a half mumble while smiling.

If I didn't know her better, I'd have thought she was on drugs. She had bags under her eyes and her skin was practically translucent. The one time I asked her about it, she practically bit my head off: "Haven't you ever had trouble sleeping at night?"

Since then, I just let her alone. Besides which, drugs or now, she seemed to be in good spirits as long as I didn't accuse her of anything.

"Are you in, Olivia? I mean, I totally understand if you're not," Ian said.

At first I'd thought maybe he didn't know about my dad and the protest or didn't remember or ... I wasn't sure. But now I understood that he did and though he was excited, I knew he'd let me bow out if I needed too.

"I think it would work, but I want to talk to my dad about it first."

Cecilia shot me a nasty look as soon as I said that and then she stormed out of the garage.

Ian ignored her because even though we'd seen Cecilia's mood improve a lot lately, we both knew all about Cecilia's mood swings.

I was a little nervous about running all this by Dad, but at the same time, he'd been a different kind of guy lately and I was hopeful that he'd be supportive of me no matter what. As per usual, he showed up at my aunt's that night and I took the opportunity to ask.

"Listen ... Ian found us this gig to play but it may be something that you'd rather I not do. I told Ian I'd run it past you instead of just signing up to do it no matter what."

"Don't tell me. He wants you guys to play at a strip club."

I laughed.

"Dog fight?"

I laughed again.

"Cockfight?"

"Cmon. This is serious, Dad. I don't want to commit to something if it would make you unhappy."

"All right, what is it, Olivia?"

"It would be playing at the rally that you guys are having at the Capitol ... only ... only I'd be on the other side. As in playing for the people who are protesting against you all."

It didn't appear to hit him as a total surprise. He got a very serious look on his face and I could tell that he wanted to give a thoughtful answer and not simply react instantly. This seemed like it could be a good thing or a bad thing. Could go either way.

"Olivia, I don't want to lie to you and tell you that I am completely happy about this. But I think it is a good opportunity for you and I don't want to hold you back either."

"You mean I can do it?"

"I mean if this is something that you support, I'm glad that you are going to do it. But I hope that it's truly something you support. I hope you're not doing it simply because you get a chance for your band to play. Do you understand?"

"I guess. You mean do I really support this whole counter-protest? I don't know that I have a good answer about that, Dad."

"Which side are you on in this, Olivia? Do you want these people to keep coming into our country and taking our resources? Do you think we need some sort of limits to all of this before it gets out of control?"

"I'm not really sure. I can honestly say that I don't know either way a whole lot, but I guess I'm still young and I'm still an idealist and I like to think that we can fit everyone in here without limiting people. I guess that's what I believe."

Dad raised his lips in what I'd consider to be the slightest of smiles.

"Well, that's good enough for me. I think it's perfectly fine for you and your band to play under one condition."

"What?"

"You have to come over and say hi to me too."

It was my turn to smile and I agreed to the deal.

"Shake on it?" he asked.

I agreed and when I did, Dad spit in the palm of his hand and reached out to shake mine. I spit too and slid my gross, slick hand into my Dad and he squeezed a little too hard and I squeezed a little too hard back.

CHAPTER 29

On the day of the protest, I spent more time than I usually do primping in front of the mirror. I wasn't trying to look like some sort of girly-girl, but I also didn't want to look like a total wanker in front of hundreds of people.

Ian met me at Aunt Jennifer's house in his mom's minivan. We headed over to Cecilia's where both Cecilia and her dad were in the garage with all of the boxes of stuff already piled up and ready to load.

Cecilia seemed strangely excited and full of energy. Her father, on the other hand, seemed a little standoffish, which made it seem even more odd when he said: "Okay, I'll meet you kids out there."

I waited until Cecilia and Ian and I were loaded into the van before I asked, "Your father's coming too?"

"Yeah. I asked him to come for moral support."

Ian and I looked at one another and let an odd feeling pass between us. I can only assume that Ian felt the same thing, but we never talked about it afterward, so I'm not 100 percent.

As we approached the gold dome of the Capitol, some police tried to turn us around.

"Sorry kids, no vehicles beyond this point."

"We're one of the bands, Kamikaze Buddhist Youth." Ian said as he passed the officer a flyer that announced our performance.

The cop looked it over and searched a clipboard until he found our name and made a little checkmark.

"All right then, pull over there in that line and you'll get right in."

Ian turned the wheel and headed for a little staging area

behind a rental truck, another van, and a station wagon jammed full of musical instruments. Another cop—this one in riot gear and with a K-9 dog cop on a leash—walked circles around the rental truck and then spoke with the rental truck driver, who emerged from his vehicle and lifted the truck's back door so that the dog could jump into the back and do some more sniffing around.

"They're searching all of the vehicles?" Cecilia asked.

"Looks that way. Probably looking for bombs and drugs. Bombs for the crazy right-wingers and drugs on people like us."

As Ian said it, he shot me a wink to let me know that he actually did think my dad was nuts, but didn't hold it against me.

"That's ridiculous," Cecilia said. "This is a violation of our rights."

"What are you worried about? You have some drugs you're hiding, Cecilia?" Ian asked with a laugh.

"I just find this whole thing disgusting. That's all. If you two actually gave a damn about any of this, you would too."

At that, she stepped from the van and pulled out her cell phone as if she was going to place a phone call in private. She stood nearly a block away on the phone when the dog and handler finally got to us. I had this crazy feeling the whole time that she was trying to avoid getting sniffed on, but it turned out to be a figment of my imagination. She returned to the van before the dog was finished and walked within inches of the dog's snout as she did it.

"What was that all about?" I asked, because I couldn't help myself.

"Nothing. I wanted to have my dad bring something I forgot."

"What did you forget?"

"Just a surprise thing. Something he got me so I can do a surprise during our last song."

"What?"

"It wouldn't be a surprise if I told you."

"You're not going to cut off all your clothes with a knife, are you?"

She shook her head.

I let it drop, but to this day I'm not sure if I should have. I tell everyone that I did all I could and I've never been a person to hold onto regrets or anything, but maybe I should have pressed her on it. Maybe I should have. I don't know. I'll never know.

The cops allowed us to move on and unload our equipment next to the stage. There were other band people hanging around. Mostly older guys. A few girls. The girls were especially nice to us and I think they found us cute, though I hoped we'd rock out enough to prove we were more than pretty young faces.

Ian saw his friend across the way and told Cecilia and me that he'd be right back. We stood and watched the coming and goings of all the other bands and speakers and it seemed like everyone already knew everyone, except for us. Cecilia and I only knew each other.

The guy who looked like he was in charge was an old hippie dude with long gray hair and gray in his beard and a tie-dye shirt and the whole deal. I wondered if he knew my aunt, and made a mental note to introduce the two of them when she showed up later. That's another thing: everyone was planning on coming out to watch. My aunt, Mr. Crenshaw, some of my teachers, Nurse Joe, even my mom. I didn't feel nervous at all about that, but when I looked out past the stage at the people milling around, I felt some butterflies in my stomach. It wasn't what I'd call a sea of people, but there may have been a several dozen standing around already.

Then, I looked past the handfuls of folks hanging out next to our little stage and I saw hundreds of people across the lawn over on the Capitol steps where Dad and his group were already getting things going. You could hear echoing voices and muted cheering and there, off in the distance, I could see someone up on their huge stage. I couldn't tell from that far away if it was Dad, but I liked to think it was. Dad, up there getting everyone all riled up. Dad, living his dream of being the spokesperson for a cause. Dad, being literally looked up to on a high stage with hundreds, maybe thousands of folks cheering him on.

Back on our side, the old gray hippie guy climbed up the makeshift cinderblock steps and took to the stage and grabbed the microphone and welcomed the small crowd:

"Thank you one and all for coming out here tonight. I'm so glad that you feel passion enough about this issue to make your voices heard. And to make sure our voices are heard, I want to start out with a little chant. You can repeat after me. We all belong, that is our song. We all belong."

It was a stupid chant and the tiny crowd barely even repeated after him. It was more of a group mumble than a chant, but after he kept doing it for five or six times and egging everyone on, the crowd did start to get a bit louder. There were some college-age kids toward the front near the stage and they started getting louder, I think, as more of a joke than anything else. It seemed like they were laughing at the old guy. But even if they were doing it as a joke, it caused the volume of the whole crowd to increase and before we knew it, even Cecilia and I were chanting along.

We all belong, that is our song. We all belong.

By the end of the chanting, when everyone was hooting and hollering and whistling and clapping, Cecilia was over beside me all worked up and yelling it at the top of her lungs. I looked back to the crowd again and I don't think anyone was as passionate about it all as Cecilia. Right as the whole thing ended, I saw my aunt and her boyfriend, Mr. Crenshaw walk up the lawn. They both had big smiles on their faces and they were holding hands. My aunt waved at me and I waved back.

Then, long before I expected it, the old dude spoke again into the mic and said something that scared me half to death: "Of course, we all know that the youth are our future and I'd like to bring the future to you here and now. We'll give them a minute to set up and then I'd like you all to giving a rousing round of applause for Kamikaze Buddhist Youth."

Now that's another thing that, in retrospect, should have clued me in to something. For the longest time we had all agreed to be called Shanghai Buddhist Youth, but then a few weeks before the show, Cecilia told us we should change our band name to Kamikaze Buddhist Youth. Ian and I didn't really care enough one way or another to say no.

Anyway, the crowd clapped in dribbles and drabs and I looked over to see Ian running in our direction and grabbing our equipment and handing guitars to me and Cecilia and lugging his drum kit onto the stage.

I felt like a zombie as I lifted one thing after another over the cinderblock steps and handed them to Ian, who expertly placed them in their correct positions on stage. I felt like I was floating above myself. Like I was dead and watching myself do it all. And then, when I looked over to Cecilia, I saw that she wasn't a zombie at all, but was instead looking frantically left and then right as if searching the crowd for someone. I realized pretty quickly that she was looking for her father, and I looked too, but didn't see him anywhere.

Before I knew it, the three of us were standing on the stage in a rough approximation of the way we'd stood in Cecilia's garage so many times before. Only instead of being elbow to elbow, in the safe, little, low-ceilinged womb of the garage, we were ten feet apart from one another in the wide open air with people staring up at us and the darkest storm cloud I'd ever seen threatening us from above.

Somehow, the crowd had grown huge.

I stared out past the sea of people and couldn't see any of them. It was as if they weren't actually people, but more like when I was four years old and I'd line up all my stuffed animals on the floor in front of me and put on a magic show or something.

I heard Ian counting off "one and two and three" as he clicked his drum sticks against the side of his snare, but I hesitated for a minute as he did it and noticed that both Cecilia and Ian were off and running before I was. I hadn't even strummed the first chord on my guitar, yet. I almost started too late, but then I realized that would throw everyone off, so instead, I just sat there and did nothing and the two of them launched into Ian's song, "Once Upon a Time," without me anywhere nearby.

And then, I looked down and saw the face of my aunt smiling up at me and then Mr. Crenshaw and then I noticed another couple walk up and join them in the growing crowd.

My mom and dad stood side by side with their arms intertwined and looked at me and both smiled. Without even thinking, I jumped right into the song as if that was where I was supposed to jump in all along.

And then I felt the pull of the music and I was swept off into the sea of noise and I played like I had never played before.

We were halfway through our fourth of five songs when I spotted Mr. French coming up through the grass. By that point we may have been near a hundred people strong in the audience. It was hard to say and I wasn't counting and we were nothing close to how many people gathered around the Capitol steps across from us, but we couldn't hear them and we were in our own world and for this short time, anyway, Dad chose to join me over here on this side.

Mr. French approached the stage and as that song ended he lifted the green guitar case up to Cecilia's waiting hands and they exchanged a glance that I could only describe as conspiratorial. She laid the case at her feet and didn't bother to open it as we moved into the last song.

I don't even remember playing that song. All I remember is the expression on the face of Mr. Crenshaw changed as he stared at the green guitar case. He stared for just a second as if he were trying to remember something. And then, he stared as if he remembered everything he'd ever forgotten all at once. He turned and whispered to my aunt and then her expression turned to one of annoyance and she turned to my dad and passed the secret and his face turned as well. He then whispered to my mom and the four of them stood with angry expressions as the song started winding down. Cecilia kept a refrain going on her guitar and then transitioned into the first notes of "Amazing Grace" and told the crowd that we had a special guest in the audience.

"With your applause, I'd like you all to please welcome Jennifer Driscoll—The Blue Nun—to the stage."

My aunt simply stood and stared and didn't approach as Cecilia lifted the case onto the chair in front of her and placed the lid to the dulcimer off to the side.

That's when I noticed that something was wrong. There were blocks of something lining the case. There were wires and buttons and too many things that didn't belong.

I think Mr. Crenshaw noticed it about the same time; I saw his expression change from anger to concern.

Aunt Jennifer noticed next.

And then Dad. Dad, who immediately jumped on the stage

and flew at me and tackled me to the ground and shielded my body with his.

My face ended up buried in my father's armpit with the smell of him wafting into my nose. I caught a glance of Cecilia as she smiled and without saying a word, stepped on a switch.

CHAPTER 30

We...

Maybe I'm caught up in this idea I have because of the way I started this whole thing, but it seems like people often start wrapping up their books with the word "we." Some guy or girl opens the damn book talking about themselves: "I, blah, blah, blah" and they're off on some journey.

Then, fifty or a hundred thousand words later the writer is starting the final chapter and they're going on and on about "we" because along the journey the protagonist met someone special or several special someones. The idea being that the protagonist is now whole and not alone anymore. The POV character has spent the novel emerging from their mythical cave and they have rejoined society and found connection and camaraderie and a bunch of bullshit like that.

Truth is, though, that some stories starts with "we" and end with "I."

My ending is definitely an "I" kinda deal.

CHAPTER 31

I suppose I could take this opportunity to go into all the blood and guts that I witnessed. The kind of stuff I sometimes address in my therapist's office when she has me lie down and close my eyes and take myself to that dark day five years ago. I could talk about the sounds, the smell, the obvious tomato soup, lid-blowing analogy. But I'd rather not chronicle that here.

That belongs to me and is sacred. Sharing it in a book would somehow diminish it, if that makes sense.

I've gone on to live a somewhat normal life. I'm heading off to college this fall at the University of Iowa and most people don't think of me as "that poor girl" anymore. At least not to my face. The start of this book was the submission that got me into the Writers Workshop there, though I haven't written much over the last few years. I'm just getting back to this thing now because my therapist suggested it.

My therapist is a very nice woman. She's really helped Mom and me.

Mom is a totally different person since Dad died. Believe it or not, we get along like sisters. Our therapist says that's okay. Says that we missed out on a lot of mother/daughter bonding when I was younger but nobody says all relationships need to fit a cookie-cutter mold. Mom and I spend many nights looking like we're living some commercial for a flavored coffee drink. We sit around the fireplace with our legs tucked under us and speak this special therapy language that we learned over the last couple of years.

We don't discuss the past but mostly focus on the present.

The past is sacred.

As I recall Dad's funeral, we all drove out to the cemetery in this giant limo and stood in the rain under umbrellas that were held by young, clean-shaven, college guys—the sons of the funeral home director. Then, as I remember, though I'm pretty sure this isn't really what happened, the limo drove Mom and my aunt and me directly to this grief counselor. That counselor met with me for a couple weeks before dishing us off on our current therapist.

I also remember Dad's funeral being attended by hundreds and hundreds of jackasses and idiots. All these Freedom and Liberty Party yahoos who saw his death as some sort of rallying cry. Although, because it wasn't some illegal alien that killed him, their rallying cry was more of a rallying whimper. The Freedom and Liberty Party movement pretty much fizzled out at the next presidential election when nobody took them seriously anymore.

Ian was also there at the funeral. He stood with his family and didn't stand with mine.

The rounded bandages at the ends of his arms—the place where his hands had once been—looked so out of place on him. I remember staring over Dad's casket, staring at Ian's bandages. Flesh-colored mittens missing the thumbs, is what I kept thinking. Why the hell couldn't they find black bandages? Something that would not stand out so much against his black suit. Something that wouldn't wrestle my attention away from Dad and mom and aunt.

Despite his injuries, Ian went on to attend Julliard as he'd planned. He was outfitted with prosthetic hands and could manage to make some music on some instruments. Mostly he studied musical theory, though. He e-mailed me recently and said he received his degree this spring and is engaged to a wonderful girl named Emily.

I'm very happy for him. And Emily. Really.

It became pretty obvious that things weren't going to work out between the two of us because too much had happened.

I spent a couple years mostly locked away in my aunt's house with my aunt, my mom, and Mr. Crenshaw, who really is no sort of perv, but a truly nice guy. When I wasn't having those flavored-coffee moments with Mom, I pretty much stayed in my room and wrote and read. I went to school and got good grades and kept my mouth shut.

Hmmm … what else?

I know that my therapist wants me to write about Cecilia. I know she wants me to come up with some nice little thing to write about her that will help me heal before I go away and find myself on my own a couple of hours drive from home.

But I really don't have anything to say.

I already wrote all this crap about Cecilia there in my room during the years following her suicide, her assassination of Dad, her murder of innocent children and men and women and old people at that rally on the Capitol steps. None of which made any sense. How could it? She didn't even target the Freedom and Liberty Party idiots that she hated so much. Except for my Dad, she basically blew up a bunch of people that she considered good guys.

I think Cecilia was simply a very sad person. I think she had always been very, very sad. I think her father was sad too, though he died there next to the stage and nobody could ever pin down how much of it all was his idea. When they found Cecilia's diaries and writings at her house, nothing mentioned or implicated Mr. French. In fact she actually wrote about planning everything by herself. She wrote a lot about Saint Cecilia, the patron saint of music. Saint Cecilia, the saint who was hard to kill. They tried to boil her alive and when that didn't work they tried to chop her head off. Three times they tried to decapitate her, but she got away. Eventually, though, three days after the last attempt Cecilia died and became a saint.

Whatever.

This shouldn't be about Cecilia anyway. This should be about Dad, who was a jackass and a drunk and then a recovering drunk and a bad father and a nutjob and a kook and bastard and a crazy lunatic and a bad husband and a poor provider who somehow rallied all these other jackasses together to fight against something that didn't warrant anyone fighting against it in the first place. Dad, who had Short Man Syndrome and a Napoleon complex, and never shied away from a fight.

This should be about Dad, who smelled of whiskey and cigarettes when he cuddled me up and held me tight and protected me from everything. Protected me from evil and badness and people who lacked souls.

This should be about Dad. This whole thing should be about Dad. Should have been about Dad all along. But no matter how hard I tried to make it that, I couldn't pull it off.

I just couldn't do it.

THE END

B. BILLY CURTIS

ABOUT THE AUTHOR

B. Billy Curtis was born and raised in Iowa. His first memory involves pounding on his grandfather's artificial arm with a toy hammer after his grandpa lost the arm in a corn picker accident.

He currently lives in a junky little shack on a busy urban street in Seattle with his wife and two daughters, a big garden and a yard full of chickens.

Made in the USA
Middletown, DE
15 January 2016